The Silver Door

The Silver Door

TERRY GRIGGS

RAINCOAST BOOKS

Vancouver

Raincoast Books acknowledges the ongoing financial support of the Government
of Canada through The Canada Council for the Arts and the Book Publishing
Industry Development Program (BPIDP); and the Government of British Columbia
through the BC Arts Council.

Editor: Lynn Henry
Typesetting: Teresa Bubela
Cover and interior artwork: Cynthia Nugent
Cover design: Ingrid Paulson

NATIONAL LIBRARY OF CANADA CATALOGUING IN PUBLICATION

Griggs, Terry
  The silver door / Terry Griggs.

ISBN 1-55192-685-7
  I. Title.

PS8563.R5365S54 2004   jC813'.54   C2003-906946-X

LIBRARY OF CONGRESS CONTROL NUMBER: 2004090367

Raincoast Books
9050 Shaughnessy Street
Vancouver, British Columbia
Canada, V6P 6E5
www.raincoast.com

At Raincoast Books we are committed to protecting the environment and to
the responsible use of natural resources. We are acting on this commitment
by working with suppliers and printers to phase out our use of paper produced
from ancient forests. This book is one step towards that goal. It is printed on
100% ancient-forest-free paper (40% post-consumer recycled), processed chlorine-
and acid-free. It is printed with vegetable-based inks. For further information,
visit our website at www.raincoast.com. We are working with Markets Initiative
(www.oldgrowthfree.com) on this project.

Printed in Canada by Webcom

10 9 8 7 6 5 4 3 2 1

For Jessica, Zachery, Megan
and Cassidy

Table of Contents

One

Murray Sheaffer, handsome, clever and rich (yes!), with a comfortable home and happy disposition, seemed to unite some of the best blessings of existence ...

Olivier paused. Or rather, it was the fountain pen he was writing with that paused, and the sentence that had been taking shape so nicely now trailed off in a frustrated splatter of ink.

"Go on," Olivier urged.

I can't, wrote the pen, who *was* named Murray Sheaffer, and who was indeed handsome — well, not bad-looking, anyway — and who was certainly clever enough to have a mind of his own. (The "rich" part was pure fiction.)

"Why not?"

I'm stuck. Blocked.

"Again?" sighed Olivier.

You've no idea how difficult it is! This writing business, a torment, sheer agony.

"Maybe you shouldn't make yourself the hero of the story." Olivier glanced over the pages of the fresh new notebook they'd been working in. Murray had decided that it was time to write a great work, his magnum opus, but he was having trouble getting beyond the first sentence. The notebook was beginning to look more like an action painting than the first draft of a book. Lines were stroked out or scribbled over, and there were doodles and drips, splotches and splashes of ink everywhere. Olivier thought his pen friend had come up with some very promising first lines but ... *Call me Murray*, savagely crossed out. *For a long time Murray used to go to bed early*, ditto. *In a hole in the ground there lived a pen* ... surely the start of a fantastic story. It even sounded familiar.

Why ever not?

"I don't think that's how it's done. I mean, you're supposed to invent the hero. Make him up."

Make someone up? Some cheap plastic twit with a rolling ball for a head? Ridiculous. Besides, it's my book and I want to be in it.

"I tell you what, Murray. I'll have a look in the one Sylvia gave me. There's bound to be some advice in it on how to start a novel."

Ah, I'm wise to your tricks, my boy. You just want to get back to reading that blasted thing. Do you realize that you've hardly done anything else in the last week?

"Not true." It was, though, and Olivier knew it. The book was hard to put down. At times it was even impossible to put down — it seemed to cling to his hands with a magnetic force. The volume in question, *Enquire Within*

Upon Everything, had been given to Olivier by Sylvia de Whosit of Whatsit, his step-step-stepgramma. Sylvia, only recently married to his gramps, had invited him to stay at her house, Cat's Eye Corner, for the summer holidays. The place was huge and fascinating — a mansion packed with oddities, surprises and mysteries. He'd only been with them for a week, and already he'd had some pretty wild adventures and had met some very unusual individuals — Murray being one of them. Olivier didn't think there was even the slightest chance that he would ever be bored here, but Sylvia had given him the book just in case. And what a book! For one thing, the title was in no way misleading. It contained information on absolutely any subject you might want to look up, and on many more you'd never dream up in a million years. Ichthyology. Aztec calendar stones. Genghis Khan. Zoroastrian fire temples. Hippies. Some information it didn't even completely contain, which Olivier discovered when he checked out the entry on Mount Vesuvius and a puff of smoke escaped from the picture of the volcano in the book, and then from the book itself!

This puff of smoke didn't disperse, either, but began drifting around Olivier's room. It sidled over to the window, skated along the ceiling, then dropped down right in front of him, forming itself before his eyes into different shapes — a spider, a smoke ring, a zeppelin, a question mark, then a hand that waved goodbye, its thumb hitchhiking toward the door, where it streamlined itself into a long, sinuous ribbon that slipped through the keyhole. Olivier ran to open the door and poked his head out into the hallway just in time to see the smoke, shaped like a frisbee, chasing Bliss down the hall. (Bliss was one of the Poets, what Sylvia called her cats, of which she had a great many.) Interesting, you had to admit, so it's no wonder that Olivier found the book hard to resist. Even at night, when Murray was tucked up in his pen case, sleeping soundly, a cuddly plush eraser by his side, Olivier lay awake, hands itching to seize the book. If he listened very very carefully, he could even hear it. It made a whispering and murmuring sound, a low hum of not quite audible voices, and light seemed to seep out of its pages, too, as though its covers were the closed doors on a luminous room.

Murray understood that Olivier was becoming more and more enthralled with the book. That was partly why he had started one of his own. He needed Olivier's help to write it and figured that just such a distraction might break the spell that was being cast over his friend. But as Olivier was hungrily eyeing the volume once again, Murray knew he'd better try something else.

I say, lad, isn't it time for lunch? I'm starving, the old barrel's empty as a drum after all this work. Why don't we go downstairs to see what's cooking, then afterward explore the house a little? We haven't done that in days.

"All right," said Olivier, without much enthusiasm. Although, now that he thought of it, he was feeling hungry. He was more than a bit relieved, too, that Murray had given up on his writing ambitions for the time being. He slid the pen into his shirt pocket and, casting a longing glance at the book, headed for the door.

Running down the stairs, zooming past walls that were chockablock with portraits and maps and hanging shields and swords and shelves full of medicine jars and tins and birds' nests, Olivier began to wonder if he would even be able to find the kitchen. The rooms in Cat's Eye Corner had a peculiar habit of shifting around. Once, after much searching, he'd discovered Sylvia and Gramps having breakfast in the games room, as the kitchen and dining room both had gone missing. His step-step-step-gramma was serving waffles with a badminton racket and knocking hard-boiled eggs across the pool table with a cue. You never knew for sure, opening a door in this house, where exactly you were going to find yourself. No surprises today, though (not *yet* anyway), for as Olivier pushed through the door of the kitchen, that's precisely where he was.

Gramps was already seated at the table eating what looked like a bowl of tundra, and Sylvia was busy fixing something at the counter, although Olivier hated to think what. Being a witch (or so he suspected), she had a creative approach to meal preparation. After sampling a few of her specialties — deep-fried bubble gum, bark stew, hand cream on a cracker — Olivier had wisely offered to prepare his own meals while staying at Cat's Eye Corner.

"Hey, Gramps." Olivier sat down beside his grandfather and slid Murray into the juice glass full of ink that Sylvia had put out. She was okay, really — for a witch — and Gramps was great. He was funny, kindly and always ready with a hug when you needed it.

"By gum, it's Ollie," he said.

Gum? Olivier stared at the bowl. "What are you eating, Gramps?"

"Not rightly sure, son, but it strikes me as something a horse might enjoy."

"Olivier, would you care for a sandwich?" Sylvia had a piece of bread in each hand and was trying to grab a small, round object that was tearing around on the counter.

"Er, no thanks, Step-step-stepgramma. I don't mind fixing myself something."

"What a resourceful boy you are, dear." She smacked the slices of bread together and set them down with a sigh. "Wild onions. Very nice in a sandwich, but a bit hyperactive. I think I'll make some refrigerator cookies instead."

Uh-oh, Olivier knew what that meant. Sylvia was going to stand at the open fridge and start popping ingredients into her mouth — milk, an egg, chocolate chips.

"So, Ollie." Gramps pushed aside the bowl and picked up a filled pita bread. "Whatcha gonna do today?"

"I don't know, some reading maybe."

"Becoming a regular bookworm, eh?" He bit into the pita. "Hmph, mrhmplmphoo." He pulled something woolly and flat and longish out of the pita with his teeth. It hung down, draped over his chin, until he yanked it away.

"Looks like a sock, Gramps."

"By cracky, you're right, it *is* a sock. I wonder if we've got a pair here." He rummaged around inside the pita bread, fishing out a carrot, a piece of cheese, a hockey card. "I'll be, here it is." He plucked the second sock out and held them both up to examine them. They were deep black with star patterns on them, constellations Olivier supposed, but not ones that he recognized. "Want 'em, son? Too small for me."

"Sure, Gramps. Thanks." Olivier didn't really want the socks, which were too fancy for his tastes, but thought he'd better get them out of the kitchen before they ended up shredded in the coleslaw. Before stuffing them in his pocket, he couldn't help but notice what an unusual texture they had. They were soft as night air, and cool to the touch. Sylvia had probably been marinating them in some vile solution that was kept in the fridge.

Which she happened to open that very moment, and as she did so, a blast of arctic air rushed out, complete with whistling wintry sound effects. Suddenly it was freezing in the kitchen. Olivier hugged himself with the cold, and he could hear Murray shivering, making the empty juice glass clink and rattle.

"Goodness," said Sylvia. Then, "Ah, the mail has arrived." She caught an envelope that was swirling around in a frigid current, then slammed the door shut. "That's better." She studied the envelope. "I wonder who it's from. Would you like to eat it, or shall I?" she said to Gramps.

"Go ahead, Sylvie."

Gramps didn't seem to find this request odd, but Olivier sure did. "Eat it?" he said, teeth chattering. "Does your mail always arrive this way?"

"No, sometimes it blows in through the heating vents. Warm wishes and all that. I take it that you'd like me to proceed in a dreary, boring and mundane fashion by actually opening the letter and reading it."

"Yeah, I would. Maybe it's from my parents."

"Not likely. That one came yesterday."

"You *ate* my mail?"

"Don't worry, nothing but stale news. They miss you terribly (ho-hum). Hope you're having fun. Your uncle dropped by for a visit and his dog Henry devoured a pair of your underwear (and you think *I* have strange tastes). My dear, don't look so glum. I tell you what, why don't you open this one and read it out to us, since you *are* quite the reader these days, aren't you?" Sylvia gave him a sly look as she handed the letter over to him.

Olivier accepted the letter, his interest in it overcoming his annoyance. The envelope was large, slightly crumpled, and soiled as if someone had used it as a dinner napkin. It bore a wax seal that was impressed with a heraldic crest, that of a fly swatter crossed with a silver ice cream spoon. Wow, this has to be from some bigwig, he thought. He broke the seal and pulled out an invitation, which read as follows:

Dear Residents of Cat's Eye Corner,
We, the Lord and I, sniff sniff, *are cordially*
Inviting ourselves to Stay at Your Humble
Residence. Please Expect To Be Honoured
With our Presence soon. Sniff!
High and Mightily yours,
Lady Muck & Lord Nose

Olivier frowned. People don't usually invite themselves to stay, do they? Maybe the upper classes were different, even though it was hard to believe that this invitation had come from someone with any class at all. The card was a mess.

There was a big smear of grape jam on it, greasy finger-prints, a tea stain and a fruit fly squashed in one corner.

"Why, how delightful," Sylvia said. "What an honour."

"Friends of yours, Sylvie?" Gramps asked.

"No, dear. I haven't the faintest idea who they are."

"Well, by jiminy, I wonder what they're like?"

"I expect we'll find out before too long."

"Guess so," said Gramps, not sounding overly thrilled at the prospect.

"Step-step-stepgramma," said Olivier, sniffing the air, "I think something's burning."

"The toast!" She dashed over to the counter and began slapping at the toaster, saying, "Get out of there, go on, shoo!"

Smoke billowed out. The toast popped up, burnt to a crisp, while the smoke itself leapt off the blackened crust, skimmed across the counter and dove into the sink.

Olivier groaned. It was the very same smoke that he had somehow released from the book.

Sylvia rushed over to the sink and turned on the water. The smoke hopped out and onto the floor just in time, but she grabbed a broom and began chasing it like a big dust-ball around the kitchen, until it slipped under the door and was gone.

"Drat that thing! It keeps setting off the smoke alarm, and every time I try to catch it, it hides in the chimney."

"I'll catch it for you," Olivier said, jumping up. "I know exactly where it belongs." He didn't know quite *how* he was going to do this, but he was feeling a little guilty about letting it loose in the first place. He reached out for Murray, slid him back into his shirt pocket and headed for the door.

"Why, that's most helpful of you, Olivier. Don't you want a little morsel to eat first?" asked Sylvia. "You do like bat, don't you?"

"Um, later, thanks."

"Come see me in the garden, Ollie. I've got the goldarndest thing to show you."

"Okay, Gramps, soon as I've done this," and he was out of there, up the stairs in a flash, thinking — the book, the answer has to be in the book. Smoke removal, maybe there was some product he could use. Or maybe there was a way of tempting it back *into* the book. But when Olivier burst through the door of his room, the pesky puff of smoke was driven completely from his mind. Murray practically jumped out of his pocket, and *he* practically jumped out of his skin. The book lay opened on his bed, which was not how he'd left it, and beside it sat something that Olivier had never encountered in his life before, something in fact that he did not even believe in. A *ghost*.

Two

"I *am* not," said the ghost.

Olivier hadn't said a word. He didn't think he was capable. All he could do was stand, frozen on the spot, staring. The ghost was that of a boy about his own age, wearing faded jeans (really faded!), a pale striped shirt and old-fashioned running shoes like the kind Olivier's dad might have worn as a boy. His hair was cut in an old-fashioned style as well, with a scarcely visible cowlick sticking up at the crown.

"Stop *looking* at me like that," it said.

"B-b-but you're a a a gh —"

"I am *not*. I told you that already."

Olivier was completely at a loss. This was too weird, even for Cat's Eye Corner. He reached a trembling hand into his pocket and retrieved Murray and the notebook in which they conversed. Murray might have some idea what was going on.

Ahhhhhhhhhhhhhhhhhhhh! Run! Murray wrote, in a most cowardly-yellow colour of ink.

Run? That wouldn't be like Olivier at all. Admittedly he was frightened — it wasn't every day that you nipped into your room and discovered a ghost sitting on the bed — but he was brave enough to face this, and more than anything, he was curious. Whose ghost was it, and *where* had it come from, and *why*? Besides, now that Olivier was beginning to calm down, he realized that the ghost wasn't particularly menacing. It just sat there, legs crossed, kicking its one foot back and forth and looking extremely put out.

What are you waiting for? Go. Go! Murray's script was so shaky it was almost impossible to read.

"You're writing something. What is it?" The ghost jumped off the bed and walked over to look in the notebook. When it saw what Olivier appeared to be doing, scribbling messages to himself, the ghost began to back away, with an alarmed expression on its face. "Say, are you loopy or something? Nobody home up there?"

What?, thought Olivier. *He* had managed to frighten the ghost! He held out Murray (who didn't much appreciate it) and said, "This is Murray. He's real, I mean, he's alive."

This dubious piece of information made the ghost turn even more pale than it already was, and it backed up even farther.

"Oh, come on," said Olivier. "I don't see the problem with believing in Murray. I mean, *you're* a ghost."

"I AM NOT!!" The ghost stamped its foot angrily, but without making a sound.

Obviously he is not. He doesn't exist.

"But you're transparent," said Olivier. "I can see right through you."

"Yeah? You're pretty transparent yourself, buddy. I know exactly what you're thinking."

"I don't mean transparent *that* way. Look ... I bet I could pass my hand straight though your arm."

"Go ahead, then. Try it."

"You want me to?"

"Sure. Here." Defiantly the ghost stuck out its arm. "You'll see. I'm as solid as you are."

Hmph, mused Murray, *an illusion with a delusion. Not all there, I'd say. Heh.*

Olivier moved closer to the ghost and, gripping Murray and the notebook in one hand, raised his other one to perform this test and prove to the ghost how insubstantial it actually was. One look in the ghost-boy's eyes, though, and he couldn't do it. He *could* do it, but he wasn't going to. What Olivier saw in those eyes was determination and fear and yearning. The ghost didn't want to face the truth, and Olivier didn't have the heart to make him do it.

"Darn, I thought for sure ..." he said, swooping at the ghost's arm, karate-chop style, and stopping short just above its wrist, as if unable to proceed further.

The ghost's eyes lit up. "See? I told you."

"Sorry," said Olivier, dropping his hand back by his side. "My mistake."

"That's okay. I'm awfully pale, I know that. I've been sick lately. But a ghost? Ha, that's a good one, it really is."

"Yeah," Olivier laughed gamely. "Was I ever wrong."

"Wait, now that we've got that straightened out, there's something I want to check. Be back in a minute."

With that, their new acquaintance moved toward the other end of the room and walked straight through the wall.

See that? What a nobody! observed Murray.

"Hard to believe, eh? First that crazy puff of smoke, and now this. I wonder —" His eye fell upon the open book on the bed. "Look, Murray, the page it's at, isn't that a picture of Cat's Eye Corner?"

Why, so it is. But from a number of years ago, I'd say.

Bending over the book to study the picture more closely, Olivier saw that this was indeed the case. Although the house in the photo was much the same as Cat's Eye Corner — the turrets, the many chimneys, the widow's walk, the gargoyles and weathervanes, the ornate front door with the lion door-knocker and the wide staircase leading up to it — it somehow looked younger. The brickwork was cleaner, the paint fresher, and everything was in perfect repair. The tall trees off to one side of the house were mere saplings in this picture, and there was no sign of the garden that Gramps liked to work in, nor the topiary bushes that he kept trimmed up. There *was* a tree in the front yard that had a tire swing, its rope looped over one of the branches, but all that was left of that tree now was an old rotted trunk. Too bad, that would have been fun. None of this was remarkable. So it was an old photo of Sylvia's place — big deal. But it *was* in a book, and even though the book's title was *Enquire Within Upon Everything*, he didn't expect that *everything* was in it. Or was it?

Olivier looked more closely at the picture and noticed that one of the windows in the house appeared to be open. It was a room on the second floor, his bedroom to be exact, although you could never be sure about the identity of the rooms here, as he had certainly discovered. The peculiar thing about this open window was that it actually was open. Its curtains were rustling slightly as if in a gentle breeze.

"Murray!" Olivier said. "This isn't an ordinary picture. There's something funny going on here."

Yes, and it's just returned.

The ghost had come back in, through the closed door. It seemed puzzled. "Place looks different somehow," it muttered. "What's your name, by the way?"

"Olivier."

The ghost smirked at this. "That's a dopey name."

"Oh? What's yours, then?"

"Peely Wally."

Olivier tried to keep a straight face, but Murray was less restrained — *Haw haw haw, **Peely Wally**!*

"I don't mean to be rude," the ghost said, with a significant look at Murray, "but you two kind of give me the willies. What are you doing in my room, anyway?"

"*Your* room? This is my room. At least it is while I'm staying here."

"Can't be. You're a dream I'm having. That's it! A dream, I did feel myself drifting off a moment ago and —"

"Just a sec, I think I know what's going on," said Olivier. "You came out of my book."

"Yeah sure, and you came out of my head."

"No, but listen, um, Peely. You see the picture of Cat's Eye Corner in the book there, and that open window. That's where this room is located in the house, I think. I know it sounds nuts, but somehow you've moved from that room, the one shown in the picture, into this one."

Olivier, scoffed Murray, *how absurd. You should be the writer, not me.*

Instead of Peely Wally scoffing, too, as Olivier had expected, the ghost went over to the book and examined the picture of the house. Then he bent over, closer and closer to it, until his eye was level with the open window. He gazed in, gasped at whatever it was he saw there and stood up abruptly. He looked around Olivier's room desperately, shaking his head, disbelief marking his features.

Why, he's gone as white as a ... well, you know. He must be feeling faint. Ha. Get it? Faint?

"Oh, Murray." Olivier rolled his eyes, but to the ghost, he said, "It's true, isn't it? Don't you know how to get back?"

"I *can't* go back," Peely moaned. He sank onto the bed and buried his face in his hands.

"Why not? We can figure out how it's done. The book will tell us. Believe me, it's amazing."

"No-o-o, I can't because, because ..." Peely's voice trailed off and he glanced up, his attention just then caught by something else, his head tilted slightly as if trying to listen to a barely audible sound in the distance.

Then Olivier heard it too, and soon the sound got louder and louder. It was a car approaching the house, something that rarely ever happened here, and it was making an incredible racket. Engine roaring, horn blaring, tires squealing as it peeled down the driveway.

"Gosh," said Olivier, running to the window, "it better slow down."

Too late. There was a loud protesting shriek, as the driver slammed on the brakes, then an even louder CRASH! WHUMP!! THUMP!!!

Peely Wally leapt off the bed, eyes wide and hair standing on end. He then dove through the floor as if he were diving into a lake, and was gone.

"C'mon, Murray," Olivier said. He hadn't been able to see much from the window — a bumper thrown into the air and a tire on the loose, weaving madly across the front yard. "Let's see what's going on. Hope no one's hurt."

With Murray tucked once again in his shirt pocket, Olivier dashed down the stairs and through the front door of the house. "Whoa," he said, seeing the front half of a car mashed into a stone structure that he knew hadn't been there the day before. The car was old, the kind with huge fenders and fins. It was purple in colour and dusted with frost. Bits of snow clung to the roof, and icicles lay all around it, broken or stabbed into the ground. The structure it had crashed into was a human figure made of large, flat stones piled on top of one another, except that the top half of it had toppled over onto the car. Olivier had no idea where the stone figure had come from, but if the car hadn't run into it, it would have driven right into the house.

Gramps was at the wreck, helping first one person, then another climb out of the back seat. One was a woman, tall and thin, and the other a short, tubby man. Both had their chins tilted and their noses in the air. Olivier wondered if they'd wrenched their necks, and he ran over to see if he could help.

The woman, on seeing him, snapped her fingers and ordered, "Luggage, boy." Then she turned her attention to Gramps, saying, "I'll want this vehicle fixed by tea time."

"That so?" said Gramps. "And who might you be?"

She inclined her head slightly, to peer down at Gramps. "Why," she said, haughtily, "I am Lady Muck. *Sniff, sniff.*"

Olivier thought how very much her name suited her. His mother wouldn't let him out the door if he looked the way this Lady Muck did. The old cardigan she was wearing was out at the elbows and crookedly buttoned, the hem on her dress was coming unstitched, her rubber boots were covered in mud, her hair looked as if it hadn't been combed in years — there was a twig in it — and a number of fruit flies were buzzing around her head.

"Pleased to meet you," said Gramps, not sounding all that pleased. He turned to the tubby little man beside her. "You'd be Lord Nose, then, eh?"

The man said not a word in response, only stuck his nose — a feature of considerable magnitude — farther into the air.

Lady Muck began to rummage in the pocket of her sweater and pulled out a banana peel, which she used to dab at her own nose briefly, before saying, with a loud sniff, "You'll find the remote control on the back seat." She then addressed her companion, "Come along, dear, I believe we're expected. *Sniff!*"

Lord Nose offered her his arm and they set off toward the house, advancing stiffly and regally as if in step to a slow, magisterial music that only they could hear. Sylvia appeared at the door, a smile of delight on her face and a litter box scoop in her hand — the one she used for flipping pancakes. She received her guests with a cordial bow and ushered them into Cat's Eye Corner.

Gramps chuckled, "That's quite the pair, Ollie. They'll drown if it rains."

"No guff, Gramps. What did she mean by the remote? And what is *that*, anyway?" He nodded toward the stone structure. "Something you're building?"

"Nope to your last question. It's what I told you about earlier, the thing I wanted to show you. Don't know where it came from, or who mighta built it. It was here this morning when I came out to work in the garden, a stone man — or was, before Lady Mucky Muck ran into it."

"You know, Gramps," Olivier said, examining the figure, "it's like those cairns the Inuit build in the Arctic. Inukshuks. They use them as landmarks. I was reading about them in that book Sylvia gave me. It really wrecked the car when it fell, the front half anyway. They could have been squashed."

"Yep. But they were both in the back. See here." Gramps had reached through a smashed window and pulled out a small, black rectangular object. A remote control.

"*That's* how they drive their car?"

"Expect so. On fast forward, too." He handed it to Olivier.

The first thing Olivier noticed about the remote were the unusual buttons it had. There were seven of them, and each was a precious stone — emerald, sapphire, topaz, pearl, ruby, opal, diamond. He didn't think they were fake, either. There was no writing below them to indicate what functions they might have. Experimentally he pressed the ruby button and a rock on the ground in front of him — the head that had fallen off the stone figure — immediately exploded. It shattered into a thousand bits that pinged off the car and rained down around them. Olivier almost dropped the remote like a hot potato. It was *dangerous*.

"By gar!" said Gramps. "What'll they think of next? You better hang onto it for a bit, son. Keep our guests outta trouble while they're here."

"You sure you don't want it, Gramps?" Olivier wasn't too sure *he* did.

"It's safer with you, Ollie. I'm too forgetful. Besides, who knows," he said, with a wink, "fella gets in a tight spot, a thing like that might be of some use."

Three

Olivier couldn't sleep that night. He had a lot on his mind, and on top of that, there seemed to be a storm brewing. The thing was, the storm was brewing not outside of the house but *inside*. Even though it was a perfectly still and cloudless summer night, he heard wind whistling in the chimney, as if it were the middle of winter. A door slammed shut somewhere in the house and blinds were tapping against window frames. A cool breeze was circulating in his own room, rattling the metal coat hangers in his closet and riffling the pages in his book. He knew he should jump out of bed and close the book, but he didn't want to because then he'd have to look at Peely Wally, who was crouched in the corner, glowing faintly like an oversized nightlight.

It's kind of dreary having a ghost hanging around, especially such an unhappy one. When Olivier had run back to his room after dinner, he saw that Peely had also returned and was flipping through Olivier's book. He looked even sadder and paler than before.

"Not having any luck?" Olivier had asked, assuming that Peely was trying to figure out how to get back home to the Cat's Eye Corner pictured in the book.

"No," Peely answered very quietly, his lip trembling a little.

"Earlier you said you couldn't go back, but I don't see why not. If you managed it one way, why not the other?"

"I'll die," he said. "If I go back into that room, that's what will happen. That's what I saw when I looked through the window into my room. Me, sick in bed, dying. But I've escaped … so far."

"I see," Olivier said softly, although he didn't, entirely. The last thing he wanted to tell Peely was that the worst had probably already happened. Otherwise what was he doing here in this near-invisible form?

Now, wide awake and all too aware of Peely crouched in the corner (he had refused the offer of a bed or a sleeping bag), Olivier resolved to ask his step-step-stepgramma in the morning if she knew anything about the former owners of the house — a family, perhaps, who'd had a sick child, a boy who might have, well, given up the ghost. Poor Peely. Surely there was some answer. Maybe it wasn't too late. A medicine might be available now that no one knew about back then. He did seem to come straight out of the past, dressed like he was from some old TV rerun. I'm going to find something to help him, Olivier thought, I know there's got to be *something* I can do.

The breeze that was entertaining itself in Olivier's room clapped his wardrobe doors together a couple of times, then shook the seed-pod collection that lay on top of his headboard like a fistful of noisemakers. How was he supposed to sleep with this racket? It was almost as irritating as that Lady Muck and Lord Nose. They were terrible guests! They complained about the food at dinner (who wouldn't?), but then ate it all, noisily and greedily, without leaving anything for anyone else. They slurped and chomped, ate with their mouths open, licked their plates, wiped their faces with the tablecloth, picked their teeth with their forks, and then complained about having to eat with the servants — he and Gramps, presumably.

"Do you bowl, boy?" Lord Nose had asked, turning his formidable nasal appendage in Olivier's direction.

"Sometimes," Olivier had answered. "Do you, sir?"

"Indeed I do," he said, picking up his soup bowl and firing it at the wall. "See?"

Sylvia's best china and he had smashed it to bits. Yet she had only laughed lightly, happy to indulge the eccentricities of his lordship.

Lady Muck had then fixed a glittering eye on Olivier and ordered, "That pen you have in your pocket. I want it."

Olivier was appalled. "Sorry," he said.

"Don't be pert. Hand it over. *Sniff.*"

"Um, no. I can't."

"My dear, we mustn't be impolite," Sylvia said, her voice steely.

Olivier appealed to Gramps, who gave a little nod, and said, "She won't keep it long, son."

Sure enough, when Olivier reluctantly handed his friend over to Lady Muck, the first thing Murray did was blast her with a stream of ink. She ended up with a large purple splatter on her dress (it was dirty, anyway), her hands were stained green and her face was covered in bright blue freckles.

"What a filthy, stupid, wretched instrument," she shrieked. "You didn't tell me it was *broken*, a useless piece of garbage!"

At this dreadful chain of insults, Murray had grown so hot that he burned her fingers and she dropped him instantly. Olivier had then snatched up his friend and, murmuring his excuses, fled from the dining room.

He glanced over to where Murray was sleeping in his pen case and almost cheered out loud thinking about the incident. What a warrior! Murray had still been extremely agitated about it when they'd returned — *The nerve of that woman! Imagine! She tried to abduct me!! And did you hear what she called me? ME, a pen of such distinction! Of course I WORK. I'm NOT a lazy, no-good aristocrat!* To help calm him down, Olivier had placed Murray's case on the pillow beside his own. He wanted to assure his friend that he was safe now, no need to worry. Olivier would look out for him.

As if privy to his thoughts, the breeze swirled around Olivier's head and then began to surf Murray's pen case over the surface of the pillow. Olivier made a quick grab for it and put it back in place. "Go away," he muttered, and it moved off into the curtains and began to rustle them.

He scooted down farther under the bedcovers, wondering about that breeze … something about it seemed very familiar … and then there was a light knock on the door.

"Yes!" he said. "I knew it." He leapt out of bed, ran over to the door and pulled it open. A girl was standing there. She had dark, windblown hair, a few strands of which were licking around her neck, and a friendly, intelligent face. "Linnet."

"Hi, Olivier." She grinned at him. "Thought I'd drop by and see what you were up to. Been hearing a few rumours."

"This is great. Come in."

She entered the room and immediately the breeze that had been playing in the curtains rushed over and curled around her, billowing the sleeves of her silk shirt and twirling her hair, lifting it back from her face. Linnet was another of those unusual people that Olivier had met during the first few days of his stay at Cat's Eye Corner. She was a wind-worker, someone who had all kinds of air currents — zephyrs, squalls, tempests — at her beck and call. She more or less took this talent for granted, although her powers never failed to amaze Olivier. He should have guessed earlier that the winds prowling through the house were hers.

He closed the door partway behind her and asked, "What have you heard?"

"That you have some uninvited company."

"Do we ever," he groaned. "Or wait, maybe you mean —"

"The ghost?"

"Shhh, he's very sensitive on that point. He's in denial."

Linnet looked around. "Denial, eh? He must be *seriously* in it, because I don't even see him."

"Gee, he's taken off again. You must have frightened him. I never knew ghosts were so nervous. This Peely Wally is, anyway, he's a real scaredy-cat."

"Speaking of cats, the Poets were having a conference when I went past Sylvia's sitting room."

"Business?"

"Sounds like they *mean* business — they're upset, mad as hornets. I listened at the door for a sec, and the room was just buzzing. Somebody had threatened to smack Emily with an umbrella, and somebody else had aimed a kick at Eliot. Not only that, Sylvia's locked them in her room because those same somebodies are supposedly allergic to cats. And to poetry. They don't like it, either."

"Are they ever asking for it," said Olivier, referring to Lady Muck and Lord Nose. He filled Linnet in on the guest situation in the house, making particular mention of Murray's defiant act at dinner.

"Good old Murray. How is he?"

"His pride is a bit hurt, I think, but he's not losing any sleep over it."

Linnet laughed, looking over at the pen case, where Murray was dreaming away about quaffing tankards of rich, foamy ink and signing his name lavishly to huge royalty cheques.

"I guess we shouldn't wake him, he looks so comfortable. But Olivier, listen, you're dressed for action — as usual." (Olivier had this peculiar but very useful habit of sleeping in his clothes.) "Why don't we go and let the cats out and see what happens?"

"Excellent idea." Olivier rubbed his hands together. "The fur is really going to fly."

The two friends were on the verge of doing this very thing, too, when something extraordinary and terrible happened — and it happened so fast that they hardly had time to think.

"Goodness, look!" Linnet was attracted by something she spotted on Olivier's dresser. That's where his book lay open, and out of the depths of its pages two tiny hands had appeared. Olivier turned, expecting to see the ghost, but instead saw a very small figure hoist itself up out of his book. It scrambled out and stood for a moment on the dresser, blinking and gazing around. It was a tiny monkey, no larger than a toy figure. "Aw, it's cute," Linnet said.

Cute it may have been, but what happened next wasn't.

The monkey's gaze fell upon Murray, and in an instant it climbed down from the dresser and up onto the bed. It snatched Murray up out of his case, leapt off the bed, skirted around Linnet and Olivier and sped through the opening in the doorway.

"No!" said Linnet. A gust of air rushed up around her.

"Stop!" shouted Olivier, and they both took off in pursuit.

The little creature was too fast for them. It zipped down the length of the hall and through another doorway at the end that also stood open. Murray must have thought he was having a nightmare. Halfway down the hall, they began to pass exclamation marks of distress, splashed onto the floor in shocked fluorescent colours. Just before they got to the door, it slammed shut, and as Olivier grabbed at the knob in panic, turning and yanking, it came right off in his hand.

"No, oh no," repeated Linnet, and she began pushing hard against the door with her shoulder, while the winds that had followed her buffeted and shook it.

Olivier was so frustrated that he felt like crying. That wasn't going to help Murray much, though, so he took a deep breath and tried to think what to do.

"We could take the stairs down and nab the monkey if comes out on the first floor," suggested Linnet.

"In *this* house? Not likely. We have to get through this door, Linnet. Who knows where it will lead, but it's the only way, and the sooner the better." He tapped his foot on the floor, thinking. "Okay, I have it."

"What?"

"I'm going to blast it open." He fished in his pocket and pulled out the jewelled remote control.

"With that thing?"

"Stand back and you'll see."

Olivier pointed the remote at the door and pressed the ruby button. Instantly the door shattered. They both ducked and held their arms over their faces as chunks and splinters of wood flew around them.

"Wild," said Linnet, shaking slivers out of her hair. "Where did you get that?"

"Tell you later …" Olivier tried to dash through what he thought was the open doorway, but only ran up against another barrier. "What's *this*?"

Linnet walked up and put her hand on it — smooth metal that was so cold it could have been made of ice. "It's … another door, pure silver by the looks of it. No handle on this one, either. You'll have to use that gizmo again."

"Right, we've got to get through." Olivier took a step back and once again pointed the remote at the door and pushed the ruby button. This time, nothing happened. He pushed it again. Still nothing.

"Try another button, Olivier. Hurry."

"I don't know what the other ones do. I could try, but we might be sorry."

"Do we have a choice?"

"Maybe I can help," came a voice from behind them.

They turned and saw that it was Peely Wally who had spoken. Linnet's eyes grew a little rounder taking him in, but she tried not to look too alarmed.

Olivier quickly introduced his friend to the ghost (How do you *don't*, Linnet almost said!), and explained how Murray had been stolen from right under their noses and how they desperately needed to get through this door to rescue him.

Peely only shrugged and said, "Shouldn't be a problem, if it can be opened from the inside. I don't know why, but I can walk through solid surfaces now. It's strange."

Olivier and Linnet exchanged glances, but kept mum.

Peely then stepped up to the door — the silver was highly polished, reflective as a mirror — and walked through it. A moment later the door slid open, and Peely stood within a small, dimly lit compartment, a bashful smile of triumph on his face.

"Yay, that's the *spirit*! That is —" Linnet bit her lip, but fortunately Peely was too pleased with his success to notice her gaffe.

"An elevator?" said Olivier. "I didn't know there was an elevator in Cat's Eye Corner."

"What's an elevator?" asked Linnet.

"I'll show you." Olivier nodded toward the opened door and they both stepped in just as it was about to slide shut once more. Before it did, something dark and feline-shaped slipped in behind them, easing itself through the merest crack before the door completely closed and the elevator began a rapid plummeting descent.

Four

The descent seemed endless. At times the elevator moved rapidly downward, and at others it slowed almost to a halt. The light within flickered on and off, as did their conversation. Olivier explained to Linnet what an elevator was (she *had* ridden on one before in their last adventure, but it didn't look at all like this one) and how people usually clammed up when they were riding in one. This was exactly what he felt like doing when he looked at the indicator panel above the door and saw that they were zooming past floor 2,489. Holy smokes, he thought, are we headed to the centre of the earth?

"Why do they clam up?" asked Linnet, although she didn't feel much like talking herself.

"It has something to do with moving vertically instead of horizontally. That's the theory, anyway. Peely, what's wrong?"

Peely was not only speechless, he was squeezed into a corner, teeth chattering and eyes bugging out. "Ghost."

He pointed a trembling finger toward the opposite corner of the elevator.

Olivier marvelled at this. A ghost afraid of a ghost — who would have thought? He was getting used to the idea of ghosts himself, so surely one more didn't matter. When he glanced into the dark corner, though, it wasn't a ghost he saw.

"One of the Poets," said Linnet, moving over to it. "Poe? How did you get in here?" She reached down to pat the young cat's head. "Eek!" She had put her hand right through the creature. It came apart, drifting upward in swaths, dispersing like …

"Smoke," said Olivier, with a groan of recognition.

It gathered itself together into a hovering and somewhat dingy grin, while Olivier filled them in on the smoke's story, where it had come from and the trouble it had been causing in the house.

"What's it doing?" said Peely. The smoke had reformed itself into a feline shape and was curling around his legs.

"I think it likes you," said Linnet.

Peely smiled. "It does, doesn't it? Hi there, little smoke. If you're going to tag along, maybe you should have a name. Smoky? Or … how about Puff?"

The smoke immediately sank into a blob shape.

"Spot?" said Peely.

Nuisance was more like it, Olivier thought, but he was glad all the same that Peely had found something to cheer him up and take his mind off his own troubles. If only he himself felt more cheerful, and hopeful. He was terribly worried about Murray. How was he ever going to find him, and when was this elevator ever going to stop? And where on earth — or *in* the earth — were they going to find themselves when it did?

"It might not want to be stuck in a name," suggested Linnet.

"Maybe not." Peely watched as the smoke changed into a jellyfish bobbing in the air, then a rat scurrying around, and then a monkey that scrambled up his leg and settled on his shoulder. "You know, that reminds me, the monkey that you said stole your pen, it was probably an ink monkey."

"A what?"

"I was reading about them in that crazy book of yours, just before you came back from dinner. Ink monkeys. They're really small, about five inches high. There was a picture of one. The book said they're also called pen monkeys because scholars in China used them to prepare their ink and pass them their brushes and even turn the pages of their books. They slept in the scholar's desk drawers, or in the brush pots. They're supposed to be extinct, but if our smoky friend here came out of that book like you said, then so could …" Peely's voice grew very quiet. "It's my fault, then, what happened. I left the book open at that page."

"It's not," said Olivier. "How were you supposed to know? Illustrations don't usually come to life and climb out of books, do they? Lucky you weren't reading about fire-breathing dragons. Now we have some idea of why it took Murray. We just don't know *where*."

"I think we're going to find out," said Linnet.

They heard the elevator squeak and creak as it finally came to a stop. A bell then rang lightly — *ding* — and the door slid open. Nobody knew what to expect, and even the smoke slid behind Peely's legs, where it quivered anxiously and shed wisps. When they peered warily out, what they saw was indeed alarming. They had arrived at what looked suspiciously like the waiting room in a dentist's office. There was boring art on the walls, uncomfortable plastic chairs lined up underneath, a coffee table laden with old magazines (some from the Middle Ages!) and a large reception desk in the centre of the room.

A woman leapt up from behind the desk and trilled, "Children, come in, come in, oh this is wonderful, *wonderful*, you're going to have so much FUN!"

"Fun?" said Olivier. He was the first to venture out of the elevator, the others following behind uncertainly.

Even though the woman was obscured by the desk, Olivier had to squint to take her in, for she was very loudly dressed in shocking pink and lime green, and her hair was a bright Pomeranian colour, and her earrings blinked off and on like Christmas lights, and her over-large purple-framed glasses flashed in the light, as did her big teeth.

"Yes indeed, fun fun FUN!!" she shrieked, as she emerged from behind the desk and approached Olivier. She held out to him what seemed to be a poster of some sort. "My card."

Taking this in both hands, Olivier read:

> **OSCARELLA VIVID**
> "She's so very THERE"
> CEO
> ADVENTURES UNLIMITED

"Once you've signed in — naturally there are a few hundred forms to fill out — we'll be able to start your adventure. Why, I have your itinerary RIGHT HERE." She rushed back over to the desk and retrieved a large briefcase in which she rummaged around, tossing out papers left and right. "Yes, YES, here IT IS!" She held up a document of considerable thickness. "Now, let's see, a trip to a shoehorn museum, my, that will be fun, and then we'll go to a fungus farm to watch the mushrooms grow, EXCELLENT, then YES, to the beach to count some grains of sand, won't that be *thrilling*, your little friend there certainly could use a bit of sun, he IS pale, isn't he, and after that, LUNCH at a school cafeteria, I believe they'll be serving their specialty, the Dreaded Breaded Bran Burger, SO nutritious, and NEXT, you'll LOVE this, we'll take in their four-hour math class, extremely loooong division, you know, EDUCATIONAL and yet so *stimulating,* and for the rest of the afternoon, you just won't get over this, a MOVIE, about drywall if I'm not mistaken (and I NEVER AM!) starring Brad Bland —"

"Excuse me, Ms. Vivid." Olivier had to interrupt before she put them all in a coma.

"Yes, YES?"

"You have the wrong group." He walked over and handed her back the card. "We're not here for a tour."

"NO?! But, BUT …" Surveying them all in disbelief, She noticed that Peely's knees seemed to be smouldering, and announced sternly, "Good HEAVENS, children, there is absolutely NO SMOKING in this room!"

Peely smiled weakly.

"NO SMIRKING, either. Can't you see the sign?" She indicated a wall on the other side of the room on which there was a sign depicting a pair of smirking lips within a big red circle with a red line slashed through it. There were several other similar signs, too, indicating forbidden activities like running, dancing, singing and laughing.

"I'm not doing either," said Peely. "This is a … pig?" The smoke, which had been drifting apart during that endless recitation of hers, pulled itself smartly together, complete with snout, trotters and curly tail.

"And NO PETS."

Olivier and Linnet exchanged a look that said, *Let's get out of here*. Linnet surreptitiously indicated a door off to their left, and Olivier nodded in agreement.

"Also NO TALKING BACK. NO JOKES. NO NON-SENSE. NO TIME TO LOSE. NO DAYDREAMING. NO SLEEPING ON THE JOB. NO MONKEY BUSINESS."

"As a matter of fact," Olivier said, "that's why we're here."

"Pardon ME?"

"Monkey business. You haven't seen one, have you? Running past your desk, perhaps?"

"Why NO, not at ALL." She had grown quite flustered, her face bright red. "I didn't see a little MONKEY, carrying a PEN, of all things! How RIDICULOUS. NOT ME, HA HA."

"No, of course not. Thanks, Ms. Vivid." Olivier glanced at Linnet, giving her the go-ahead. She raised her fingers to her lips and whistled, as if calling a dog.

"OH!" said Oscarella Vivid, for all of a sudden the papers in her open briefcase began to fly out of it, one after another until a mass of them were swirling around the room, caught in a great gust of wind. She screamed in alarm and began to run after them, jumping up and trying to snatch them out of the air.

"Peely, this way," said Olivier. Linnet was already at the door and over the threshold.

"Children, no, NO. DON'T GO IN THERE. IT'S NOT ..."

And that was the last they heard, before they fled through the open door and it slammed shut behind them.

Five

The walls were smooth and very cold to the touch. Marble, Olivier thought, or even glass. It was difficult to tell for sure, as it was so dark. They had been running down what seemed to be a long corridor, their footsteps echoing beneath them (except for Peely's). Given that they must be miles underground, he had expected that they'd find themselves in something more like a tunnel or a mine shaft, dank and hot. The air here, though, was fresh and cool and smelled slightly sweet, like cotton candy.

Fortunately they weren't completely in the dark, as Peely was emitting his usual low-level glow and providing just enough light to make their way forward.

"Where do you think this is taking us?" said Linnet, finally slowing down the pace to a quick walk.

"Got me." Olivier slowed down, too, to catch his breath. "I just hope we're headed in the right direction to find Murray."

"There was only one other doorway in that reception room, so we have a fifty percent chance of being right."

"Great. What do you think Peely? You're awfully quiet."

"You expect me to be rattling my chains?" he said, then added, more seriously, "I may not be rattling mine, but I think someone else is."

"What do you mean?"

"Can't you hear it? In the distance … that sound. A clunking, banging sort of noise, and then a roar, like an ocean or something."

Olivier stopped for a minute and listened closely. "You're right. I guess there's only one way to find out what it is."

"No, there *is* another way," said Linnet. "I can send a scout ahead to snoop around. It can't tell us what's up ahead, but it will give us some sense of whether it's dangerous or not."

So saying, Linnet clapped her hands together twice, sharply. Olivier then felt a rush of air flowing over him as a bolt of wind sped up the corridor, and away.

They walked on in silence for a while longer, until Peely observed, "It's getting lighter. Must be some lamps up ahead."

"Yes, and louder," said Olivier. The banging sound that had at first been so faint was now more alarming. It seemed to be the thumping, crashing noise of something very large hitting the ground, like a giant's footsteps approaching. This sound was followed every time by a roar of … what? It reminded Olivier of the time his dad had taken him to a baseball game at the SkyDome. The stands had been packed, and during the game the crowd seemed to speak with a single tremendous voice.

With a chilling howl and a moan, the scout was back and began rocketing around and around, scrambling Linnet's hair, flapping and billowing her clothes. Peely had to duck aside before he was blown away, and the smoke that had been riding on his head like a puffy baseball hat, slid down the back of his shirt before it was scattered entirely.

"Calm down, it's all right," said Linnet soothingly. "That's it. Good work."

"What's up?" asked Olivier.

"Not sure. But we'd better be careful. There definitely is some danger ahead."

"Look at this, on the floor," said Peely, who had crouched down to avoid the wind. "It's … it's … *blood*. Jeepers, let's get out of here. This is crazy, let's go back! We can go on that tour with What's-her-name. It'll be boring, but at least we'll be *safe*."

"Oscarella?" said Linnet. "No thanks."

Olivier moved over to Peely and crouched down beside him. He stuck his finger in the splatter of blood on the floor and held it up to examine it. "Ink," he said. "Red ink. We're on the right track … but he must be hurt!"

"Maybe just angry," said Linnet. "Seeing *and* spitting red."

"He'll be *that* for sure. Peely, you can turn back if you don't want to go any farther, but Murray is my friend and I'm going to find him no matter what." Olivier didn't add that of all of them, Peely was the one who was most likely beyond harm and had the least to fear.

"A *pen*? You're going to risk your life for a measly *thing* like that?"

"He's *not* measly. Don't say that. Don't you have any friends?"

When Olivier saw the pained look on Peely's face, he knew the answer to that one, and continued quickly. "You *do*, you have us, and so does Murray, and we're going to rescue him. You with me, Linnet?"

"You bet."

"Peely?"

Peely stood up, gazed longingly down the corridor, then conceded. "Might as well. I can't go back home, anyway."

"Good. Let's see what's going on up ahead, but we've got to be very very quiet."

The children moved forward cautiously, and it wasn't long before they came to a large room that was filled with cages and prison cells, all of which were empty. There were a couple of staircases leading up to trap doors in the ceiling, and a lift operated by pulleys that likewise led to another, larger trap door. As well, there were ramps leading outward to other corridors and rooms. It appeared to be a holding area of some sort.

"Might be a circus," suggested Peely. "These cages could be for the animals."

"That's true," Olivier said, wandering over to one of the cages to take a closer look.

A loud CRASH sounded directly above, followed by a tremendous ROAR. They all gazed up at the ceiling.

"I don't like circuses," said Linnet. "Clowns give me the creeps, and the animals have to perform dumb tricks."

"The animal penned in this cage left behind a teddy bear," said Peely.

"Maybe it wasn't an animal. Or not a four-legged one." Linnet's tone was grim.

"I didn't think of that."

"Okay," said Olivier, "who wants to check out one of those trap doors? If it's lifted up a crack, we should be able to see what's going on up above, without being seen ourselves. We've got to find out where the exit for this place is."

"Be my guest," said Linnet.

"Why don't we just look down some of the other hallways?" asked Peely. "There has to be more than one way out."

"And get totally lost? I don't know … I suppose you could try it, but I want to find out what's happening up there. It'll give us a better idea of what we're dealing with and what to do next. So, I guess I'm volunteering for the trap door, eh?"

"I'm right behind you," said Linnet.

"Me too," said Peely, none too keen to go off exploring on his own.

Without giving himself too much time to think about it, Olivier headed for the staircase on the left side of the room. He ascended quickly, his friends behind him (but hanging back just a little), and placed both hands on the trap door at the top. He gave a slight push to test its give, then a firmer one, which did the trick. He raised the door only high enough to peek out. "Ohhhh," he said.

"What?" whispered Linnet, behind him. "What do you see?"

Olivier didn't say anything as he continued his survey,

then he slowly lowered the door and closed it once again. When he turned around to face them, Linnet saw that his face had gone as pale as Peely's.

"*What* is it?" she said.

There was another CRASH. Another ROAR. The whole room seemed to shake with the impact.

"It's an amphitheatre," Olivier said. "Like the Colosseum in Rome. It looks exactly like the picture of it that I saw in my book."

"You mean there are gladiators and lions and stuff like that out there?" said Peely.

"No lions that I could see, but gladiators, yes, I suppose you could call them that, but they're enormous, and they're ... ah, made of stone."

"Huh?"

"Yeah, they're like stone statues come to life and they're trying to smash this poor little kid who keeps running away from them, and the audience, there's hundreds of people out there, they keep shouting for the stone men to ... it's horrible."

"Let me see," said Linnet, and she pushed past Olivier and lifted the trap door herself, but too forcefully and the door flew back out of her hand. It flapped open, landing on the wooden floor of the amphitheatre with a resounding *thud*. Suddenly they were exposed — the door having opened in a central area of the arena floor — and instantly noticed.

"HURRAAAY!!" The crowd roared, "CHILDREN, MORE CHILDREN! BAD, BAD CHILDREN!! GET THEM! PUMMEL THEM! FLATTEN THEM!!"

"Olivier —" groaned Linnet.

"Doesn't matter," he said, "we've got to get out of here, anyway. First we have to save that little kid. I'll distract the stone guys and you help her. Find a way out if you can and I'll try to follow. Peely, maybe you should go with Linnet. Peely?"

The ghost was gone.

"He must have ducked back downstairs … Olivier, watch out!"

When Olivier had first peered out, he'd seen two stone men stomping around and hurling boulders about as big as their own heads at a terrified little girl who was streaking here and there, running for her life, but managing somehow to avoid being hit. What he hadn't seen was the third man lurking behind the trap door, who now grabbed him by the hair and yanked him right out of the opening, then held him up, kicking and flailing, for the crowd to appraise. They went wild.

"SMASH HIM! CRUSH HIM!!"

Olivier felt as though his scalp was going to be ripped off his head. "Let go of me!" he shouted. "Let *go,* you big lummox!"

Amazingly, the man did, and Olivier fell to the arena floor, scrambled to his feet and took off, while the bloodthirsty audience shrieked, "CATCH HIM! MASH HIM!! KILL KILL KILL!!!"

Linnet leapt out onto the floor and, although she desperately wanted to help Olivier, she instead tore across it in the opposite direction to where the little girl was cowering behind one of the boulders that had been thrown at her. She uttered something to the child, then grabbed her hand and dashed with her toward an arched entranceway where two guards, dressed very much like Roman soldiers, were standing.

By this time the spectators were beside themselves, bellowing and frothing with rage, but divided as to which young interloper they wanted to see destroyed first, Linnet or Olivier.

Olivier, meanwhile, was running circles around the gladiators. One of them was hurling rocks at him, while another had picked up a stone trident and was attempting to skewer him with it. The third followed with a sword and net. Luckily they were a lot slower than he was. Even though it was three against one, he kept them busy, distracting them from their original target while deftly avoiding the blows.

Feinting and dodging, hopping quickly aside, he even managed to make two of them crash into one another. The man with the trident got tangled in the net and then fell on top of the other one, with a loud "OOOF!" The audience groaned with frustration, and glancing up at them jammed into the tiers of the amphitheatre, Olivier noticed something odd and extremely irritating: besides being the ugliest adults he'd ever seen, they were all, every last one of them, eating ice cream cones. Towering multiflavoured cones, six and eight scoops high, were socked in their fists. The people who weren't screeching were eagerly stuffing their faces, licking and slurping. Ice cream ringed their wide-open and jeering mouths, and ran in sticky rivulets down their furiously waving arms.

"BAD BAD CHILDREN," they were chanting. "TOO NOISY! TOO MESSY!! NO DESSERT!!!"

Olivier frowned and clenched his jaw. It just so happened that his favourite treat was ice cream, and he was very hot at the moment from all the running and exertion, and he hadn't eaten anything much during that whole day at Cat's Eye Corner, and the people in this crowd were so unbelievably cruel and greedy that he thought, Cripes, I've had enough! He reached into his pocket for the remote (which, to be honest, he'd forgotten about until now). He wasn't quite sure what he was going to do with it — he didn't want to stoop to their level — but perhaps everybody here could use a demonstration, a little boulder-blasting to show them what they were dealing with — not some helpless kid.

The problem was, Olivier had paused a fatal second too long and wasn't paying close enough attention to the movements of the third gladiator, who had approached him from behind. He was knocked to the ground, and the stone man who had first picked him up by the hair towered over him. Olivier flipped over in an attempt to leap back up, but was then pinned, as the man placed an enormous foot on his chest. He couldn't reach his remote, and he was afraid he was going to be squashed like an insect, which was certainly what the audience was screaming for.

Olivier stared up at the man, at his hard, grey features, and was surprised to see his look returned. The gladiator's eyes were alive in a face of stone, and incredibly they radiated sympathy and intelligence. Almost imperceptibly the man inclined his head and indicated with his eyes that

Olivier should look in the direction that Linnet had run. A murmur of astonishment rippled through the audience, and when Olivier did look, he saw why. Linnet had used her wind powers to pick up the two guards by the portal and twirl them in the air, spinning them around and around, as she raced past them and through the arched doorway with the little girl.

Then something even more surprising happened, something that caused the audience to fall completely silent — at least for the amount of time it took them to absorb the shock. Peely appeared, rising directly through one of the other trap doors without even opening it. Clearly he was determined to help Olivier, but because he was terrified, he was also wavering more than usual, flickering in and out of visibility. His expression was ghastly, and there even appeared to be smoke pouring out of his ears as he marched across the arena floor. The *sight* of him was so uncanny that everyone in the audience was scared silly. When they finally found their voices, they began to scream and moan, but this time in fear for their own lives, rather than crying out for someone else's.

"OHHHH, NOOOOO! A GHOST! HELP US! SAVE US!! A GHOOOST!!!"

Peely stopped and looked around. "I *am* not," he muttered. "Geez, is everyone blind?" Then he shouted, "You, hey you! Get your foot off my friend."

The gladiator's lips twitched as he tried to suppress a smile and lifted his foot. Olivier immediately jumped up and, giving Peely a thumbs-up, said quietly to the stone man, "Thanks. You could have easily finished me off."

The man nodded, and said in a deep, rumbling voice, "Go."

By this time Linnet had re-emerged alone at the arched entranceway. She raised both hands in the air and the sawdust that covered the arena floor (it was there to soak up spilled blood) began to swirl up in great clouds and drifts as if a sudden sandstorm had hit the amphitheatre. Linnet directed most of this at the audience, and once again the raucous crowd began shrieking and yelping as the sawdust got on their ice cream and in their eyes and stuck on their faces and hands.

Olivier motioned urgently to Peely and they both streaked toward Linnet, the smoke trailing in their wake. The guards who had earlier tried to stop her were still dizzily staggering around and had no inclination to block her exit this time. Together they slipped through the doorway and down a long foyer that led outside to an empty street.

"The little girl?" asked Olivier, as they hurried along.

"Safe," said Linnet. "Let's go. It won't be long before that mob picks the sawdust out of its teeth."

They began to run and then quickened their pace, going full throttle as they heard the roar of the fumbling crowd in the amphitheatre grow louder and angrier.

Six

Olivier's sense of unease didn't lessen any as they flew down a street crowded with shops and houses and low apartment buildings, most of them brightly painted and cheery enough, but troubling all the same. This was because of the signs hanging in windows and posted on door fronts that caught his eye as he ran past ... NO CHILDREN ALLOWED and ADULTS ONLY and NO DESSERTS, BUT JUST DESERTS and THE HANSEL & GRETEL B&B, CHILDREN EATEN FREE!

"Did you see *that*?" he said to Linnet. "Why d'you think these people hate kids so much?" He was glad that the streets were deserted, the cranky citizens of this place presumably all in the amphitheatre.

"Don't know. Not everybody does, though. When I took the little girl outside there were a few people hanging around who were all right. I mean, they were so sad and worried and were wringing their hands and pacing up and down, and then when they saw her, they were overjoyed. She ran to them and got hugs and everything, so I figured she'd be safe with them. They were really grateful, too, but scared, and they hustled her away before I could ask them what was going on."

"I don't like it. Let's just find Murray and get out of here." Except how on earth were they going to do that? Needle in a haystack, he thought, trying to keep a sharp eye out for clues as they ran down the street. The place was vaguely Roman in appearance, but in a theme-park sort of way, with numerous columns and friezes on buildings that were covered in alabaster and marble. There were statues that seemed more like live models holding poses, and caryatids that looked as though they could step down off their pedestals and walk away, leaving the building they were supporting to crash down behind them.

Olivier would have been thrilled if he were in a real ancient Roman city, but he didn't think that every second or third store in such a city would be selling ice cream. Variety stores, cafés, ice cream parlours — all had displays in their windows (the glass here looked too modern as well) advertising fantastic ten-scoop cones — each scoop a different flavour — and magnificent ice cream cakes, and luscious sundaes that were drizzled with chocolate, butterscotch and strawberry syrups and decorated with nuts, wafers, marzipan and cherries. At one point Olivier had to backtrack to find Peely, who was standing transfixed in front of one of these window displays, gaping at a laden banana split.

"Peely, we can't stop," he said, at the same time feeling an almost irresistible urge to stare at it, too.

"I wonder why it doesn't melt," said Peely dreamily.

There *was* something strange about these desserts. Olivier looked away, and then down at the ground, determined not to be lured in. "Oh, hey, what's this?"

Peely tore his gaze away from the window. At first he couldn't see what it was that Olivier was pointing at in the dust. Then he said, "Tracks. So? It's only pigeons — or, no, they're not bird tracks, they're … monkey tracks? The ink monkey!"

"You weren't the only one wanting that banana split."

"My favourite dessert," Peely sighed. "When I was well enough to eat."

"Something tells me you wouldn't want to eat that one. I don't think it'd improve your health any. Let's scram. I can't even see Linnet now, and we've got to stick together."

**

With her usual breezy swiftness, Linnet had run ahead and soon found herself outside of the city in a field overgrown with tall grasses and plants in full bloom with orange and blue and purple flowers as big as plates. Pausing to glance back, she saw that she'd outrun the others, and decided she'd better wait for a bit to let them catch up. To keep herself amused, she stirred up a wave of wind that rushed through the grass, combing it first one way, then the other. This made a lovely *shushing* sound. The flower heads nodded up and down. Linnet yawned, and before long her own head began to nod. She motioned the wind back, then directed it to swirl and shape and tie knots in the grass directly behind her until it had made a springy green chair that she settled herself in very comfortably. The air smelled so fragrant and agreeable that it reminded her of her home. She lived in a boat that was set way up in the trees in the woods near Cat's Eye Corner, and at night gentle winds drifted through the branches, rocking, rocking ...

G!

Linnet's eyes flew open. *What was that?* Darn, she thought, I just about drifted off.

L!

She jumped up from her grass chair and looked all around, but didn't see anyone who might have spoken. She didn't see the others, either, and wondered if she had been asleep, and if so, for how long. But surely they would have seen her, or called her.

O-O-O-O-O!

Now she could hear a thumping kind of music.

RRRRRR-I-A! G-L-O-R-I-AAAAAAA!

"Oh!" A huge bee zoomed in front of her face, where it hovered briefly before flying over to one of the flowers. This bee was followed by several others, and they were the ones who seemed to be making the music and singing, instead of buzzing. They were rocking and rolling and bopping around in the flowers with such abandon that it wasn't long before the bees' striped bodies were covered in little leisure suits of pollen, and it was stuck thickly on their feet like platform shoes.

G-L-O-R-I-A-A-A, G-L-O-R-I-AAAA!

"Gloria? That's not my name."

N-O? N-O W-A-Y?

"No way," she laughed.

T-H-E-N, H-E-Y H-E-Y H-E-Y, W-H-A-T D-O Y-O-U S-A-Y?

"It's Linnet."

Y-O, L-I-N-N-E-T!

"Who are you guys?"

W-E'-R-E N-O-T T-H-E B-E-E-T-L-E-S, H-A H-A H-A!

"All right, let me guess. Umm, okay, you like to sing so you could be Song Bees?"

N-O N-O N-O.

"Hang on, give me a sec. You're not Honey Bees, I guess, or Bumble Bees. Humming Bugs? No wait, I *know*, I've got it. You're Spelling Bees!"

Y-E-A-H Y-E-A-H Y-E-A-H!

Linnet was thrilled, and she couldn't wait to tell Olivier. It seemed he was always the one who claimed to have had a conversation with some animal or insect and she never believed him (or at least teased him by pretending not to).

"Say, you haven't seen my friends, have you? A boy about my height ... well, *two* boys actually, although one is, um ...

O-U-T-T-A S-I-G-H-T!?

"That's one way of putting it."

S-U-R-E T-H-I-N-G, L-I-N-N-E-T. F-O-L-L-O-W U-S.

The whole time that Linnet had been talking to them, the bees had been jiving and dancing around, some in the flowers and others right in front of her eyes, but now they all gathered into a tighter group and sped off. If Linnet wanted to follow, and she knew she'd better, then she was going to have to rely on the wind for a ride — not something she would normally do when travelling with the others. It didn't seem fair, and besides, she didn't want to resort to her special powers too much and grow lazy and forget how to do things herself. There didn't seem to be any choice at the moment, though. Olivier and Peely must have headed in a completely different direction. She went to work and quickly summoned up an air raft (one made entirely of air) then climbed aboard. Soon she was stretched out flat on the raft and skimming over the tops of the long grass, plumes tickling her arms and legs, and dodging around flower heads so big they surely would have knocked her to the ground if she'd hit one.

Linnet kept the bees in sight, and she could hear them singing in the distance as they zigged and zagged along. They were heading due north — at least she thought so, as the air was getting chillier. Eventually she left the field behind and passed over a small stream and into a wooded area. She was surprised that the other two had come this far, and was beginning to wonder how *much* farther it was when she spotted a familiar trickle of smoke weaving like a garland through the branches of a tall, bushy pine tree above which the bees were circling. As she arrived at the spot and jumped off the raft, they rose up, gathered themselves back into a formation as dense as a whole note, and spelled out the longest word she'd ever heard: H-O-N-O-R-I-F-I-C-A-B-I-L-I-T-U-D-I-N-I-T-A-T-I-B-U-S. They spelled it twice more, then sang, D-O-N'-T F-O-R-G-E-T, L-I-N-N-E-T. B-Y-E B-Y-E. S-O L-O-O-O-O-O-N-G!

"I won't. At least I'll *try* not to, whatever it means. Thanks, you guys," she shouted after them as they headed back toward the field.

"Linnet! I thought that was you. Who were you talking to, and *where* were you? We've looked everywhere. What was that noise, anyway, it sounded like a radio?"

It was Olivier who spoke, poking his head out from between the branches of the pine tree. And, boy, *was* he upset — but more with himself than anything. On top of losing Murray, he thought he'd lost Linnet. They hadn't been able to find her in the field and had set out to look for her elsewhere, but in the wrong direction, he just knew it. Peely had been whining and snivelling the whole time and Olivier, exasperated, had finally told him to "drop dead." He honestly couldn't believe he had said that, and had tried to explain to Peely that it was only an expression, it didn't really mean anything. He and his friends said it to one another sometimes, but nobody took it seriously.

"That was the Spelling Bees you heard, they're so funny, wait'll I tell you," Linnet said, but then added, "later." Olivier appeared to be scowling at her. "I think I must have dozed off while I was waiting for you two to catch up. Sorry. You're not mad, are you?"

"'Course not." He managed a weak smile.

"Whew."

A light wind flickered around him, soothing as a gentle breeze, lifting his spirits.

"I'll make sure we don't get separated again. Where's Peely?"

"In here." Olivier ducked back behind the branches of the tree. When Linnet followed, she saw that the overhanging branches formed a bower within, a cozy sheltered space underneath the tree that was carpeted with layers of fallen pine needles and large enough for three or four people to gather in. She also saw Peely huddled against the trunk of the tree, and was shocked at how faint he'd grown. He seemed to have made himself as small as he could, and was seated with arms wrapped around his legs, forehead pressed against his raised knees, shivering. He reminded Linnet of a weak candle flame that was about to gutter out.

"Peely, what's wrong?" she said.

"Nothing," he mumbled into his knees. "I'm cold, that's all."

Olivier went over to him and crouched down. "Look, Peely, I didn't mean to be grumpy. No food, no sleep, that's the problem. Would these help warm you up?" He reached into his pocket and pulled out the socks that Gramps had given him. Strangely, the socks were no longer black with star patterns, but sky blue with a big blazing sun covering one ankle.

Peely glanced up. "Yeah, maybe. I'll try them. The more I think about that banana split we saw, and I can't seem to stop thinking about it, the colder I get. I know I

was being a pain, Olivier. Everything's my fault, you two
would be better off without me."

"That's not true," Olivier said. "Don't forget that
you're the one who helped us escape that crowd in the
amphitheatre. You terrified them."

"I did, didn't I?" Peely smiled to himself, as he undid
his running shoes and tried on the socks. "These *are* warm."

"They remind me of wind socks," said Linnet. "Which
are perfect for summer, except they have a habit of blow-
ing off your feet. And they're hard to catch sometimes
in the morning when you're getting dressed. Where'd you
get them?"

"In a pita bread Gramps was eating."

"A sock sandwich? You know what, I'm so hungry I
could eat one of those myself right now."

"Me too," both boys agreed at once.

"So, what's the plan? We've got to get our hands on
some supplies before we continue hunting for Murray."

"There's a place not far from here, a store of some kind
that Peely and I discovered when we were looking for you.
It might have something."

"We don't have any money, or whatever they use here
to buy things with."

"I can sneak in and swipe something," offered Peely.

"I don't know about that, but let's go have a look at this
store, anyway," said Linnet. "Then we'll figure out what to
do. Let's be *wary*, though. Remember, kids are an endan-
gered species here."

Seven

Olivier, Linnet and Peely were crouched behind an old-fashioned claw-footed bathtub that was abandoned in the yard, off to one side of the store. The smoke had trailed after them when they left the pine tree shelter behind, but was now nowhere in sight. Good — they didn't want the smoke to give away their presence in the yard, while they tried to figure out exactly what kind of store this was, and whether or not they should steer clear of it. It was a ramshackle three-storey building, made of fieldstone and brick and wood and this and that. A sign hanging crookedly out front read:

Uncle Truckbuncle's Odditorium
~~No~~ Children welcome

"What's an odditorium?" whispered Linnet, peeking over the top of the tub.

Olivier whispered back, "I was hoping you'd know. I wonder why that 'NO' is crossed out? Do you think children are welcome, or not?"

"Has to be a trap," said Peely.

"Probably."

"There isn't even a front door on the hinges," said Linnet. "That makes it look welcoming enough, but once you're inside, watch out."

"Quiet," Olivier warned. "Someone's coming out."

They grew perfectly still as an elderly man stepped out onto the sagging front porch of the building and peered around. First he looked intently one way, then another, as if he were about to cross a street, then he raised a small ebony spyglass to one eye and gave the yard and the trees all around an even closer scrutiny. The children were afraid to breathe or make even the tiniest of noises, as it seemed obvious that the old man knew there were trespassers — *young* ones — on his property.

What happened next, though, caught them off-guard. The man turned back toward the door opening, signalled to someone still inside the store and gestured for them to come out. A young boy appeared, carrying a bag in his hand. He gave the elderly gentleman a hurried hug, then leapt off the porch and sprinted away, down a path that led into the woods on the other side. The man watched until the boy was gone and then turned to go back inside, but not before saying aloud, "I'm out of doors, at the moment. Heh, little joke there. I've got lots of neat stuff inside if you kids are interested. Lunch, too. Come on in if you want. You're safe here."

"What do you think?" asked Linnet, as they watched him disappear through the entrance. "I've definitely heard better jokes."

"Could still be a trap. A set-up. That kid might have been working for him," said Peely.

"That's possible, I suppose, but he sort of reminds me of Gramps," said Olivier. "I think he's on the level." He stood up. "I'm going in. Just me for now, in case I'm wrong."

"If you're not back in five minutes, I'm coming after you," said Linnet. "Don't forget you've got that remote gizmo in case there's trouble."

"Right," Olivier gave his pocket a pat as he set off across the yard.

He climbed the steps to the porch and entered the store. He found himself in a large room that was dim and shadowy despite the light that was spilling in through the front door. When his eyes adjusted to the gloom, he saw that there were shelves reaching up to the ceiling all around, and on those shelves were all sorts of interesting objects. A hasty survey revealed an antelope's skull, a Tahitian drum, a linstock, a ship's model, a conch shell, a glass jar full of jade thumb protectors (for archers), a brass bell, a canoe bailer, an elephant incense burner, a feathered sceptre that looked like a big duster, and a bamboo nose flute (the ideal instrument for Lord Nose!) — all definitely oddities and just the sort of inventory you'd expect to find in a shop called an odditorium.

At the far end of the room the elderly man was seated at a large desk, examining a thick book that was illuminated by a gooseneck lamp. He glanced up from the book and smiled. "Ah, son, so you've decided to come in. Welcome, welcome." He stood up and extended his hand, saying, "Name's Arthur Truckbuncle, but you can call me Uncle. And you are — ?"

"Olivier." He walked over to the desk to shake Uncle Truckbuncle's hand, which felt warm and dry in his own. "Pleased to meet you, sir. How did you know we were outside?"

"Spyglass, it's a good one."

"Truly, if it can see through things." Olivier didn't find this too hard to credit, as he himself was certainly familiar with objects that had unusual powers. (Also, the three of them might not have been as well hidden as they had thought.) "Nice store." He looked up at the crowded shelves again. "Are all these things special, like the spyglass?"

"In their own way. Is there anything you're looking for, anything I can help you find?"

"There *is*." Maybe, he thought, just maybe … "A pen. A very unusual fountain pen."

"What make?"

"His last name is Sheaffer."

"Writes music?"

"Sometimes. When he's had too many bottles of ink."

"I know the family. Don't have any on hand, I'm afraid. Let's have a look in the dogalogue, shall we? Maybe I can order you one."

"Dogalogue?"

"Yep, let's see …" Uncle Truckbuncle began to flip through the book that he'd been reading when Olivier came in. "First name Murray, by any chance?"

"Yes!"

"Missing, it says. Not available. Now, I can get you a Cuthbert or a Hortense."

"No, no, they won't do." Olivier felt let down but tried not to show it. "He was stolen right out of my room by a little monkey, an ink monkey we think it's called."

Uncle Truckbuncle frowned. "Why, that would be Pistachio. He's been a terrible nuisance lately, stealing everyone's pens, even their pencils. The Emperor's up to something, along with his usual nasty somethings, that is."

"The Emperor?"

"Of Ice Cream, yes. Ahh, here are the other two. Come in, come in."

Olivier was dying to ask who this emperor was, and more about the monkey — his first solid lead! — but he waited while his friends introduced themselves. They had ventured into the store and were glancing nervously around. When he hadn't returned outside, Linnet, true to her word, had come to check on him, with Peely trailing anxiously behind.

"I bet you're all starving," said Uncle Truckbuncle, slapping his hands together. "I'm going to prepare a picnic. We can have it right in the middle of the store here, so why don't you look around while I go out back to the kitchen and get things ready. I don't have rules about not touching the merchandise, either. Go right ahead, feel free. I'll answer your questions, Olivier, once we've had a bite to eat. Some grub, by cracky!" he said, as he shuffled off.

"Grubs, ew," said Linnet. "D'you think he'll try to poison us?"

"Not a chance," Olivier smiled. "By cracky."

"Hey, I could use some of this." Peely had wandered over to the shelves, and now held a jar in his hand. "Bronzing cream, gives the skin a healthy warm glow, it says. Should I try some? It might make me look, you know, better. Heathier, more like you guys."

"You look fine, Peely. You could try it, if it makes you feel better," said Linnet.

"Only a little, to test it first," warned Olivier, knowing that's what his mother would say.

As Peely opened the jar and rubbed a dab of the preparation on his arm, Linnet and Olivier also began to peruse the shelves. Linnet spent some time admiring an elm longbow, a silver hunting horn, then a plate with the blue figure of Zephyr, the wind god, painted on it. Olivier tried on a French lancer's cap, trailed his fingers over an old matchlock pistol and plucked at the strings of a zither. He then put the conch shell to his ear to listen to the ocean, and instead heard someone say, "We cannot take your call right now, please leave a message at the sound of the foghorn." Hastily he set the shell back on the shelf.

"Do I look terrific, or what?" said Linnet. She had put on a beautiful sparkly jacket, studded with jelly beans and gumdrops, with smarties for buttons. "It's a Sugar Coat," she laughed. "That's what the tag says, anyway. Come see, there's a whole rack of oddball coats here."

Olivier walked over just as Linnet held up a sloppy jacket with specks of toast and cookie crumbs flying off of it — perfect for Lady Muck, he thought.

"A Coat of Crumbs!" Linnet said. She pointed to another that was soft and grey and looked a bit fuzzy.

"A Dust Jacket? Ha. Get a load of this hot pink one. It's supposed to be a Coat of Paint." He touched the sleeve. "Tacky."

"I'll say. What's this? It's got flames bursting out of the armpits. A *Smoking* Jacket. I should have guessed."

"Speaking of smoke, where's our pesky little friend?"

"Maybe it finally got lost," said Linnet. "Hey, Peely … you look, um, *wow*, how much of that stuff did you smear on?"

"Not that much." He grabbed one of the coats from the rack and hurriedly put it on, trying to cover himself. He had turned a bright BRIGHT orange. "A little goes a long way, I guess. I didn't *know*, do I look that bad? Say, this coat's inside out. It's a great fit, though."

"Yes, unfortunately it is a very good fit." Uncle Truckbuncle had returned with a tray that was heaped with sandwiches and goodies and a big pitcher of fresh lemonade. He stared sadly at Peely for a moment before setting the tray down in the middle of floor on a worn Persian carpet, similar to the one that Sylvia had in her sitting room in Cat's Eye Corner. "It's a Turncoat, son. Why don't you hang it back up and we can all tuck in, eh. My, my, that is quite the tan you've got there. A real peculiar shade. Oops, sorry, no pun intended, heh."

Everyone sat down on the carpet and got to work on the sandwiches, including Peely, who had turned an even brighter shade of orange out of embarrassment. Olivier noticed, though, that for all his show of appetite, Peely only seemed to haunt the food — he didn't actually eat anything. He would hold a sandwich up to his lips, then put it back on the plate with a slight grimace. Maybe he couldn't eat.

"I believe you have some questions you want answered?" said Uncle Truckbuncle thickly, after he'd polished off his fifth peanut butter and honey sandwich.

Olivier was trying to decide between a butterscotch brownie and a lemon square. "Lots. Who is this emperor you mentioned? And the monkey? Pistachio, did you say … that's his pet? If you can tell me where he lives, then I can get Murray back." He reached for the brownie *and* the lemon square, which was more or less stuck to it anyway.

"What I want to know," Linnet said, "is why everyone here hates kids?" She told him about what they had witnessed in the amphitheatre. "Even that sign out front of your store says 'No Children Welcome.'"

"Horrendous," he said gravely. "I'd heard rumours about the goings-on in the city, but I was hoping they weren't true, that things hadn't gone that far. He *has* to be stopped. Her too, his wife, she's just as bad. They've become tyrants. He's poisoned people's minds, turned them against their own children. That sign, somebody came along and painted the 'No' on, and I crossed it out."

"But how? How could parents not like their own kids, or be made to?"

"Incredible as it may sound, I think there's some secret ingredient in the ice cream he sells. It's poisonous, but not in the usual way. He's the Emperor of Ice Cream, remember. He started out small, only had a little cart he used to wheel around, but then he stumbled upon some formula, at least that's what I suspect, because suddenly people couldn't get enough of the stuff. But the more they ate of it, the more selfish and miserable they became, and the more wealthy he grew. Next thing you know he's got himself a big ice cream palace and starts calling himself Emperor, and not long after that, children begin to disappear."

"And no one cares," said Peely very quietly.

"Some do, son. There are some parents who resist, and who hide their children, and not everybody eats the stuff. At least we're not being forced to, yet. That day is coming, I'm afraid."

"What about those stone guys, which side are they on?" asked Olivier. "That one in the amphitheatre helped me, you know. He didn't want to hurt me."

Everyone expressed surprise at this, even Uncle Truckbuncle. "You don't say? Well now, that's interesting. A Shuk? That's what they're called, by the way. I thought they were all under his control, same as the ink monkey."

"Ow! This cake is pretty stale, Uncle. I almost broke my tooth on it," said Linnet, holding her jaw.

"That's not a cake," said Olivier, taking it from her and scraping off the chocolate icing. It was an object he'd recognize anywhere. "It's a hockey puck."

"Is *that* what it is? Couldn't figure the darn thing out," said Uncle Truckbuncle. "Even tried to open it with a can opener. You might as well keep it, lad, might need it where you're going."

"Where's that?"

"North. In fact, that's the *only* direction you can go here any more. I'll show you."

The old man got up, a bit creakily from sitting crossed-legged on the rug, and hobbled over to his desk, where he delved into one of the lower drawers, rustled among some papers, then returned with a scroll. When he had seated himself again and unfurled the scroll, they saw that it was a map, and on it there did seem to be only one direction — north. The compass drawn in one corner of the map pointed in four directions, but an N was indicated after each of the arrows, instead of the usual W, S and E.

"That doesn't make any sense," said Olivier.

"True. Another of the Emperor's brilliant ideas. All roads and paths, and hopes and desires for that matter, are supposed to lead to the Ice Cream Palace."

"What a cheat. But easier for us, I guess, since we have to go there."

"As long as we can get away again," said Linnet.

"Yes, you must be very careful, even travelling there," said Uncle Truckbuncle. "You see here, beyond these woods, on the main road, that's Mrs. Kidd's cottage. *Don't* go there whatever you do, no matter how tempting it seems. She is a friend of the Emperor's and has been implicated in a number of the disappearances. Once you're well past her place the road diverges, and you should take this more roundabout way." He pointed to a winding passage through a low range of mountains. "You'll come to a wide river, see here, it's called the River Stynx, thanks again to the Emperor. The effluent from his ice cream factory behind the palace pours into it — and be sure not to get any of that stuff on you. You'll have to find a way across. There are daily tours, of course, but being children, you'll want to avoid those."

"What I *want* is to go home," said Peely, his voice shaky.

"You —" Olivier started to say, intending to offer some reassurance, something he felt he could use a healthy dose of himself at the moment, when he heard that very word echoed by someone who was standing in the open entrance of the front door, briefcase in hand.

"YOOOOOOOO HOOOOOOOO, CHILLLDRENNN! Why, there you ARE, you little RASCALS!!"

"What the heck?" said Uncle Truckbuncle, clutching at the map as he got to his feet.

"Not *her*," groaned Linnet.

But it was. Oscarella Vivid surged into the room, her accessories blinking and flashing, as was the huge smile on her face. "Come, come NOW, kiddies. We're a little LATE to see the famous DRUGGED SLUG MARATHON, but I don't think we've missed TOO much! GRACIOUS, what a kitschy LAMP," she said, meaning Peely. "Did you get IT at a yard sale?! I just LOOOOVE ORANGE, don't YOU!! Okay, kiddiwinks, no stalling now, it's TIME to GO!!"

It most certainly was. They all mimed their dismay and cast each other meaningful glances. Shrewdly, however, she had their escape route blocked, and was holding her briefcase in a menacing way, as though she might actually bop them one if they tried to sneak past her.

Olivier scanned the room to see if there was an uncluttered window they might be able to leap through, and saw instead, on the shelf directly opposite, their missing puff of smoke. It was pouring out of the spout of a silver teapot and making a beeline for Oscarella.

"OH! OH DEAR!!" she said, as the smoke wrapped itself like a hive around her head. "HELP! FIRE!!" She tried to brush the smoke away but it clung to her, filling her eyes and mouth. She began to cough and sputter and stumble around.

"Don't worry, miss, I'll go fetch a pail of water," offered Uncle Truckbuncle, winking at the children as they fled out the front door, waving at him and shouting their thanks.

Olivier stopped before jumping off the front porch and ran back in to give the old man a hug as the young boy before him had done.

"Take the tub," Uncle Truckbuncle said to him.

"Pardon?"

"The one out front. You'll need to push the emerald button to get 'er started. Good luck, son."

"How do you know — ?"

"Better go."

"Okay, got it. Thanks again, Uncle. That was the best picnic I've ever had."

Olivier ran out of the Odditorium and dug in his pocket for the remote. He hit the emerald button, and immediately the old bathtub leapt to attention, its claw-feet pawing the ground, raring to go. Linnet and Peely stared at it in surprise, but when Olivier jumped in the tub, they followed right after. As the thing roared out of the yard like a hot rod, kicking up gravel behind it, they could still hear Oscarella crashing around in the store and saying things like, "I JUST wanted to touch base — OOH! EEEE! Location, location, LOCATION, AHHHG! Have a NICE DAAAYYYY!!!"

Eight

The ride was bumpy, but what a riot. As the tub scrabbled and clattered along on a road made of inlaid stone, they gripped its sides tightly and hooted with laughter. It was like being on a wild ride at the fair. They shot past farms and houses and through villages, scaring up flocks of birds, making dogs bark, and causing people to shout and shake their fists after them. At one point an odd creature took up with them — it looked like a cross between a wombat and a beaver. It ran along behind the tub for some distance, gasping and snorting and sneezing, until finally it veered off into a swampy area and was gone from sight.

Even though their pace was too fast to observe the country in much detail, Olivier did notice that there was a lot of garbage lying around — used dixie cups and milk shake cartons rolled across the road, and discarded ice cream wrappers swirled up in their wake. All of the buildings they passed were crumbling and derelict, with boarded-up windows and crooked shutters and front yards overgrown with weeds and sprawling ivies. Anyone would think these places had been abandoned for years, but Olivier spotted lots of people out front of them lounging in chairs, snoozing in hammocks or playing slow, lazy games of catch or tag. All adults, too, and all resembling the kind he had seen in the amphitheatre — swinish and sticky-faced, with the unmistakable air of bullies. There wasn't a single child to be seen anywhere.

They might have travelled along in this unusual manner for some time, heading farther and farther north, if the tub hadn't become smitten with a yellow rubber duck, some kid's bath toy that was lying abandoned on the side of the road. No one else even noticed the toy, but all at once the bathtub screeched to a halt and ambled over to the shoulder, where it began to hop around excitedly from foot to foot. Its passengers were getting seriously bounced and jounced.

"Ohhh, I'm beginning to feel seasick," said Linnet, climbing out.

Olivier followed right after, intending to see what the holdup was. "Aha!" He picked up the rubber duck. "Guess our tub wants this. Stands to reason."

"I wish it *would* stand … still, that is," said Peely, who had remained inside the tub and was hanging onto it as if it were a bucking bronco.

"Here you go." Olivier placed the duck in the tub, which responded by making a deep gurgling sound of appreciation.

Next thing, though, it *did* go. It reared up on its hind legs, dumping Peely in the middle of the road, then took off on the run, heading back the way they had come.

"Hmph. We've lost our ride," said Olivier, as they all watched it scramble and clatter away into the distance. He tried pressing the emerald button on his remote to see if that would bring it back, but the tub only went faster.

"Dumb tub," muttered Peely, rubbing his backside.

"It saved us from you-know-WHO," said Linnet. "Besides, we might be closer to our goal than we think. There's a crossroads up ahead, with a signpost. It should give us some idea of how far we still have to go."

"Yeah, *walking*," grumbled Peely as he followed behind the other two. They were both eager to see what was on the sign, which pointed toward four different locations.

"Nonsensia," read Olivier when he arrived at the signpost. "Funny name for a place."

"Uck? There's a town called Uck?" said Linnet.

"Dullsville. Bet you that's where Ms. Vivid is from."

"The Ice Cream Palace, straight ahead," said Peely, coming up behind them. "No contest."

"Precisely. Who'd want to go to those other places?"

"And it's the closest," said Olivier. "Ten longueurs, whatever that is. While the other places are hundreds of longueurs away. That sounds fishy to me. Like there's only one place you could easily get to in this country."

"Sounds more than fishy." Peely had turned around again, brow furrowed, concentrating. "Sounds like trouble, listen."

Olivier and Linnet both spun around and squinted anxiously down the road. They didn't see anything, but they could hear a rhythmic booming noise in the distance. Muted at first, it was getting louder by the minute and was clearly heading in their direction.

"Thunder?" said Linnet.

"Don't think so. Quick, this way."

Following Olivier, they ran to the side of the road and jumped into a shallow ditch. Luckily there were some low, scrubby juniper bushes growing there that concealed them — more or less — as they crouched down and made themselves as invisible as possible (which was much easier for Peely to do, even though he was still as orange as a pumpkin). They waited as the sounds grew louder … BOOM, BOOM, BOOM … and finally what came into view was a troop of Shuks. They were marching heavily along, about twenty of them, their faces expressionless, their pace steady and unvarying. What was most alarming about this procession was that in their midst, chained like convicts, were three children, two girls and a boy. They looked terrified and exhausted as they trudged along, chains clinking on the road. Their faces were dusty and smudged from crying, and their clothes ripped and out at the knees, as though they'd been in a scuffle. Which they no doubt had, thought Olivier. He could barely restrain himself from jumping out of the ditch and doing something desperate to try and rescue them.

What stopped him was one of the Shuks, who was marching at the very end of the column. As he passed their hiding place, the stone man turned his head toward the bushes and stared through them, directly at Olivier.

It was the *same* man who had spared his life in the amphitheatre, and now he was frowning and shaking his head slightly, but warningly, as if to say, *Wait, not yet, this isn't the time for rash acts.* Olivier nodded and the group moved on, steps thudding loudly as they moved up the road toward the Ice Cream Palace.

"I thought you said they were good guys," said Linnet, the sharpness in her voice making the bushes rustle fiercely.

"One of them is," said Olivier. "Maybe more than one, but they would've been outnumbered in that bunch."

"Did you see those kids?" moaned Peely.

"We'll help them," Olivier said, determined. "But we've got to see what we're up against first, or we'll end up being prisoners ourselves. Hush, someone else is coming."

Sure enough, a figure was running up the road from the direction of Dullsville. It was a man dressed all in black — shoes, pants, turtleneck — and wearing a pair of mirror sunglasses and a black beret. As he ran along with a dancing, shuffling sort of step, he was also snapping his fingers and crooning what sounded like *eeee, oooh, doo-wah, doo-wah*. Given this, they thought for sure the man was going to take the road that led to Nonsensia, but instead he turned a sharp right and continued in the same direction that the Shuks and their captives had gone.

"The Ice Cream Palace," said Linnet, with a shudder of apprehension. "Everyone's destination."

"Including ours," said Olivier. "The coast is clear, reckon we better get going. I sure can't wait to see Murray again," he added, which helped him get his feet back on the road.

They began to walk in the direction of the Palace, expecting it to loom up ahead of them at any minute. They walked and walked, briskly at first, and then more slowly as the day began to wane, and still there was no palatial building in sight, or even any of the others who had gone ahead of them. They were growing very tired and hungry and cold, and as a consequence of all that, a bit cross.

"How long *is* a longueur?" complained Linnet.

"About a thousand miles," Peely complained in return.

"It's kilometres, not miles," said Olivier.

"Who says?"

"I do. No one says miles any more. That's ancient, something my dad would say."

"Tough bananas. Miles, miles, miles! *There*, got it?"

"Cool it, you guys," said Linnet.

"I don't have to," responded Peely. "I'm already freezing. Even my socks are snowing."

They looked down at Peely's feet. There did seem to be a minor blizzard happening in the vicinity of his ankles.

"It *is* cold, you're right about that," said Olivier, shivering and rubbing his arms. "I can see my breath."

"Me, too. No, wait. That's not my …" A long, drifting cloud of vapour appeared in the air in front of Peely's face. Except that it wasn't vapour at all. It was —

"Smoke!"

"You're back."

"Yay!"

"Good work at the Odditorium."

"Yeah, brilliant."

The smoke swirled dizzily for a minute, buoyed by the praise and the warm welcome, then settled around Peely's shoulders like a soft, flowing cloak. Everyone was cheered by its reappearance, and no longer felt so glum and weary. They continued on, night now beginning to fall, with only Peely's orange glow to guide them.

Despite their improved mood, Olivier knew that soon they would have to find some place to take refuge for the night. He didn't think that he could walk much farther himself, and he sorely needed some sleep. As they moved along, he kept a lookout for some spot that might do, even a sheltered wooded area or grove, but there seemed to be fewer trees the farther north they travelled. Finally he did see something silhouetted against the darkening sky. It was a small building — a cottage, by the looks of it — set in a field some distance back from the road. Beside it a lone tree was growing, its silhouette misshapen and almost leafless.

It didn't take much to persuade his companions to stop and check the place out, but they approached it guardedly, recalling Uncle Truckbuncle's advice about avoiding a cottage where someone named Mrs. Kidd lived. This cottage was completely dark inside and certainly looked deserted, but still, not taking any chances, they crept up to it silently and peered in through the one window that wasn't boarded up.

"Can't see anything inside," whispered Linnet. "Can't hear anything, either. Seems okay."

"The place is deserted. No sign of life anywhere," said Olivier.

"Except the tree," said Peely. "Didn't you notice? It's an old apple tree, and there's even some apples on it, way at the top."

"Dinner! It's better than nothing. Who wants to climb up?" asked Linnet.

"Not me, I'm beat. Don't think I could reach them anyhow." Olivier eyed the few apples that were left on the old, gnarled tree. "Come on, Linnet, you live in the trees."

"I know, I know," and she walked beneath the tree, nodded once, and a lively wind sprang up and gave the topmost branches a firm shake. The apples tumbled to the ground and they ran to scoop them up, one for each of them.

"I suppose they're safe to eat," said Olivier, suddenly hungrier than he could remember ever being before.

"Of course, they're just apples." Linnet promptly took a bite. "Mmm, delicious. Not dry at all."

"I think I'll save mine for later," said Peely.

"Good idea." Olivier nevertheless took a bite of his own apple, then another, and another, and in no time flat, he'd devoured the whole thing, core and all. He knew that Peely couldn't eat anything and didn't want to make him feel left out by eating the apple in front of him, but it had smelled so wonderful — and tasted even better — that he'd been unable to resist. Now he felt so pleasantly satisfied and sleepy — really sleepy, in fact — that he suggested they go inside the cottage and see what it had to offer in the way of a fireplace, or beds, or even just some blankets.

"What if it's locked?" said Peely hopefully.

But it wasn't. The cottage door opened easily, without even a creak of protest, and Olivier entered a small front room that did have a fireplace in it, although that was all it had. There were no chairs, rugs, tables, pictures, cupboards — nothing. Even though it was dark inside and they had to feel their way around, they soon discovered that this was true of the other rooms, too — the kitchen and the one bedroom in back. The place had been swept completely clean of furnishings.

"We could try to light a fire," said Olivier, yawning as he plunked down on the floor in front of the cold hearth.

"We could," agreed Linnet, also yawning, and sitting down beside him.

"I'll gather some wood," offered Peely. "Do either of you have matches?"

No one answered.

"Matches?" he said more loudly. "We'll need those, you know."

Still no response. He bent down to look at them and saw that both Olivier and Linnet were sound asleep, one slumped against the other. "Oh no," he said softly. They were *all* tired, but this wasn't right. "The apples. It was those darned apples." He still had his apple clutched in his hand. He gazed at it in horror, and then instantly dropped it. It bounced across the floor and rolled right into the open fireplace, where it glowed for a second with a cool, white light. With a yelp, Peely tore out of the cottage and disappeared into the rapidly accumulating darkness, an agitated stream of smoke trailing not too far behind him.

Nine

When Olivier awoke, he had the feeling that he'd been asleep for a long time, although it hadn't been a very restful sleep. He'd had endless dreams that were scary and frustrating. Most seemed to feature a lurking presence that he couldn't quite see or escape. It was as if he had stones for feet. In one dream he saw his friend Sylvan standing outside of the cottage and looking in, his silvery-white hair luminous in the dark, his expression worried as he said something repeatedly that Olivier couldn't make any sense of. Knowing Sylvan, he was probably trying to explain some complex chess move or a mathematical formula, but in a language that only three people in the world could understand — and Olivier wasn't one of them. He smiled to himself, wishing his friend really was here. It had seemed so real. He wondered idly if Sylvan and Linnet were getting along any better now than when he'd first met them. Linnet? Where was she? He blinked and looked around. *Where* was he?

He sat up with a jerk, wide awake but confused. He was in a room that was furnished with chairs, a table, a rug, a stool (the kind Gramps called a creepie), a fireplace … with a fire gently burning in it, giving off a faint scent of apples. The apple, he remembered, and the abandoned cottage … but surely this couldn't be the same place, for it had been completely empty.

Peely was gone, although to Olivier's great relief he saw Linnet. She was standing by the window, watching something in the yard. Or someone. Olivier could hear a voice outside, a person singing. Weirdly enough, the song he heard drifting in was a favourite of his step-step-step-gramma's, and one she often hummed while going about her business (witch's business, presumably). *Jeepers creepers*, he heard, followed by a zapping noise, then, *where'd you get those peepers* … ZAP … *Jeepers, creepers, where'd you get those eyes* … ZAP!

"She's killing them," Linnet said quietly.

"What? Who is?" Olivier got up from the floor — which took some effort, he was so achy and tired still.

She turned from the window. "You're awake."

"How long was I — ?"

"Days, I think. I don't know, a long time anyway. I just woke up, too. You were right not to trust those apples."

"Didn't stop me from eating one." He walked over and stood beside Linnet, and when he looked out, he saw the person who was singing. It was a woman, tallish, with upswept white hair, cheeks rouged, lips a bright red. She was stylishly dressed in green, and on her feet she wore narrow, sharp-toed purple shoes. She was striding around the yard carrying a pesticide canister with which she appeared to be spraying flowers. Perfectly nice flowers, too, little ones called Johnny-jump-ups that Olivier recognized from the garden at Cat's Eye Corner. She aimed the nozzle at one, singing *jeepers, creepers*, then ZAP, a vile cloud of blackish vapour shot out and frazzled the plant to nothing. Behind her back, more flowers popped up out of the earth, and singing merrily, she turned around and, *where'd you get those peepers* ... ZAP, she wiped them out too. Singing and zapping, this went on for some time, until she paused, glanced up at the window and waved. Olivier felt a chill, like an ice cube, sliding down his back.

"Mrs. Kidd," he said.

"Guess so."

"Where's Peely?"

"I don't know, but I hope he got away."

"Because we're trapped?"

"Uh-huh. The door is locked."

"Don't forget that I have the remote, Linnet. I can blast it open." He reached into his pocket. "*Gone.*"

"She must have frisked us while we were asleep."

"She even took my hockey puck."

"Never mind, we'll think of something. Hang on, here she comes."

Satisfied with her killing spree, Mrs. Kidd had set down the canister and approached the cottage. They heard her rattling some keys outside the door and stood apprehensively, waiting, as she unlocked it. The door crashed open and she breezed in, saying gaily, "Good morning, children. How lovely of you to visit. I was just doing some gardening. Wretched little flowers. They'll choke out the weeds if you let them."

"Why do you want weeds instead of flowers?" Olivier asked. He didn't mind weeds himself, but that's not the way it usually worked.

"Why," she looked surprised, "because they're ugly, a nuisance. Oh, you young people are so charming. Imagine actually liking flowers!"

"Where did all this furniture come from? It wasn't here last night, or whenever it was we got here," said Linnet.

"Questions, questions. Children *are* inquisitive, aren't they? Everything was asleep, wasn't it? Good, that's settled." She booted the door shut. "It's time for a snack. What would you like? Children are always hungry, aren't they? You're in luck, I have some yummy ice cream, a fresh supply. Lots of different flavours, too. Let's see, there's flatworm, or deadly nightshade. Also mud flavour, mummy wrapping, tuna fish, turnip, halitosis and diesel. My, what *funny* faces you two are making. Children do that, don't they? Aww, that's so *sweet*." She clasped her hands together. "Are you having trouble deciding? You're allowed to have more than one kind, you know."

"No thank you," said Olivier decisively. "We appreciate you letting us stay for the night, but we must be going now."

"What a little gentleman. I just *love* children with good manners."

"You don't like children at all," Linnet blurted out. She didn't mean to say anything, but the woman's own manner was so annoying.

"Oh, but I *do*. I love children. Especially *al dente*," she mused. "With tomato sauce and a touch of Parmesan grated on top."

Alarmed, they looked at her to see if she was joking, but it didn't seem so. She sighed happily, as if recalling some former culinary delight.

"Go!" said Olivier, and they made a run for the door. Before they could reach it, though, they both felt a sudden prickling sensation in their feet and legs. And then a great heaviness possessed them entirely. They were frozen on the spot.

"Whatever is your hurry, children? We were just getting acquainted. I tell you what. If you promise to come back where you were, like good little darlings, I'll thaw you out. Handy device, this."

They couldn't promise anything, as their lips were numb and stiff, but they heard a pronounced *click*, and almost immediately the frozen sensation drained away and they were able to move again. Walking reluctantly back into the centre of the room, they saw that the device Mrs. Kidd had used on them was the remote, which she had evidently snatched out of a big purple purse that sat open on the stool — the creepie. She kept the remote trained on them as she made herself comfortable in the armchair near the fireplace.

The opal button, Olivier thought, as that was the one her thumb was still poised over. At least now he knew what functions *three* of the buttons had. But how was he going to get it away from her before she started experimenting with the rest?

"What fun!" she said. "I have an idea, why don't we play a game, to *kill* the time, until we're all hungry. A guessing game ... or a quiz. I'll ask you some questions. I tell you *what*, if you answer all the questions correctly, I'll let you go. That's fair, isn't it? Children like things to be fair, don't they?"

"Yes, they do," said Olivier, in case that was the first question. He knew she'd try to trick them.

"Wonderful, yes, all right. Let's start with an easy one to get you warmed up. What is bioluminescence?" she smirked.

"That is easy," said Olivier (it was, anyway, for someone who had recently been reading a book called *Enquire Within Upon Everything*). "It's the production of light by living things, like fireflies or glow-worms. They contain this substance called luciferin that can produce light when it oxidizes with a certain enzyme."

"*Very* good. My, you are clever." She smiled pleasantly, or tried to — it was actually more of a grimace — and continued with the next question. "Let's give the girl a turn, shall we? Tell me, what's special about owl's feathers, hmn?"

Linnet gave her an even look. "The edges of the feathers are very soft, so they won't make any noise in flight. Makes it easier for owls to catch their prey." But you won't catch *me*, you old bat, she thought.

"Good, *excellent*, heh. Next, then. How fast do fingernails grow?"

"Two point five centimetres a year," said Olivier, without hesitation. "On average." This was just the sort of thing he happened to know.

Mrs. Kidd raised an eyebrow. "Metric, eh? Fine, I'll accept that answer. Girl, you again. What colour are snowflakes?"

Trick question, Linnet sighed. "No colour, they're clear. They might look white, but that's because of the white light reflected from the edges of the snowflake into your eyes."

Mrs. Kidd pursed her lips, and looked just a tiny bit put out. "Yes, of course. Even a simpleton knows *that*. Let's try a harder one, shall we? What is believed to be the smallest unit of measurable time?"

Olivier and Linnet glanced at one another — each hoping that the other knew the answer. *Oh-oh*, they both thought, looking away again. Linnet frowned and gazed into the fireplace at the flames gently flickering over the logs, hoping some answer might occur, but then out of the corner of her eye she saw the stool move. She could have sworn that she saw it sidle away from the armchair where Mrs. Kidd was seated, the purple purse wobbling on top of it.

Olivier, meanwhile, was staring hard at the window, thinking.

Mrs. Kidd began to chuckle. "Give up, kiddies?"

"Planck time," he blurted. "It's the smallest unit. One second contains 600,000,000,000,000,000,000,000,000,000,000, 000,000,000,000,000 Planck times." This is what Sylvan had been trying to tell him in his dream. He had given Olivier the answer — all those zeros! — in advance. Then he thought, I wonder if it *was* a dream?

Mrs. Kidd's lips were pursed very tightly until she spat out, "Yes, fine! That's *common* knowledge. *You*, Miss Smartypants." She glared at Linnet, who was struggling to stifle a laugh. "What's another word for 'honourableness'? You don't know, you ignorant child, because it's not something you'd know anything about. Children have no sense of honour, no finer feelings, the little brutes. You can't spell it, either, can you? Go ahead, just try and spell it! You don't have a clue, *do you*?"

Spell it? The bees, Linnet thought, the Spelling Bees. "Sure, I know that," she said casually, examining her fingernails, then crossing her arms, looking once again at the stool (it moved again!). Darn, what was it, what *was* that strange, long word they had told her to remember? She understood now why they had. She pictured them jiving and bopping around, and recalled that the word had a sort of rhythm to it, a pattern. Hesitantly, she started to spell it, then picked up speed once she got going, "H-o … n-o-r-i … f-i-c-a-b-i … l-i-t-u-d-i-n-i-t-a-t-i-b-u-s. Honorificabilitudinitatibus!"

Mrs. Kidd was flabbergasted.

"Wow, killer spelling," said Olivier, impressed. "We win for sure. Let's go!"

"Not so fast, young man," said Mrs. Kidd. "One last question. A giveaway, I'm sure. A bonus, easy as pie, and I do like *pie* … how many yards are there in a mile?"

"Yards in a mile?"

"Yes," she said slyly. "Imperial measure, you know."

"Nobody uses that any more." Except Peely, he thought, and my dad. He could have kicked himself. Instead of arguing, he should have found out something about it.

"Stumped?" asked Mrs. Kidd. "Not smart enough? Nothing but a stupid kid, after all? Never mind, dear. Let's have a little *bite* to eat, and forget all about our silly game. I'll even use my best dishes, my Childware pattern, it's so cunning, you'll love it."

Olivier kept his cool (even though he didn't *feel* very cool). He was sorely tempted to lunge at her, to knock her over and make a grab for the remote, which she was still holding. Linnet, too, was on the verge of either trying to whisk it out of her hand, or creating havoc in the cottage by raising a storm. Then a knock came at the door.

"Whoever can that be? I'm not expecting company." Mrs. Kidd marched over to the door and snatched it open. "Yes? It's … no one. Must have been the wind." She moved back toward the chair, the remote pointed at Linnet. "Don't you try anything funny, girlie. You, either," she said to Olivier. "Or I'll puree you both on the spot. Save me from getting out the blender."

Another knock sounded. Louder this time.

"Again?" She strode back and pulled the door open. Still no one was there. She stuck her head outside and looked around. Nothing. Irritated, and shaking her head in puzzlement, Mrs. Kidd returned once again to her chair, but before she could seat herself, there was yet another, even louder, knock at the door and she stormed over to it. "I've had enough of this prank! It's children doing it, I know it … hateful, despicable, giggling *brats,* taking advantage of a poor, helpless old woman … which is to say, not *that* old, I'm only thirty-nine, I mean twenty-nine, er, more like nineteen, if you want the truth."

More like a hundred and nineteen, thought Linnet, as Mrs. Kidd furiously yanked open the door again and let out a shriek of frustration.

"YOU DO THAT ONE MORE TIME AND YOU'LL BE SORRY," she bellowed into the vacant air. This time, after slamming the door shut, she stood right beside it, tapping her foot, waiting. Her finger was resting on the topaz button of the remote.

Olivier was getting nervous. Having watched a flash of orange skim past the window every time there'd been a knock, he had a pretty good idea of who was doing it. Peely must have been nearby the whole time, keeping a close watch on the cottage. Now he was trying to help them escape by diverting her attention. Olivier knew they had to try something, and fast, too, because if Peely knocked again he was surely going to get it. Whatever "it" was that the topaz button delivered.

Mrs. Kidd was watching the door so intently that he thought they might have a chance to jump through the window. He raised a fist, ready to smash it open, and at the same time tried to get Linnet's attention by motioning to her. For some reason she had her eye on the stool.

Then the knock on the door came, a lighter *tap tap tap* this time.

"No!" Olivier shouted.

Too late. Mrs. Kidd hurled it open and hit the topaz button. The person standing there was certainly familiar — although it wasn't Peely. It was the man they had seen earlier at the crossroads, the one dressed all in black and wearing mirror sunglasses, who had been headed toward the Ice Cream Palace. It looked as though he'd had the misfortune to call on Mrs. Kidd at precisely the *wrong* time.

"Ooo-wah, doo-wah, baby," he said. And then, "Oooh, hhheyyy man, heyyyyy what's happenin' ..." as he began to shrink. He got smaller and smaller, until he was about the size of a red squirrel.

"Don't call me a baby," snarled Mrs. Kidd. "Babies are horrid things. Smelly, noisy, useless creatures, ugh, the very thought! I'll show you, *you rodent*, playing that infantile trick on me and now calling me names." She then began to stamp her foot, trying to crush the poor little man underneath, while he ran around in circles, dodging the blows.

"Hey, cool it, will ya? C'mon, hey, stop that, I'm only the messenger, man ... yow, watch it!"

With the door gaping open, this was the moment that Olivier and Linnet should have made a break for it, but the stool beat them to it. It *had* been creeping along, just as Linnet had been observing, and now it shot toward the door as fast as its short, scrambling legs would take it. It was so eager to get out of the cottage (even Mrs. Kidd's furniture hated her, and every night she had to go out hunting for the escapees) that it scooted right under her stomping feet and sent her flying. She hit the floor with a crash, and Olivier nabbed the remote as it sailed out of her hand.

"Bad scene, man," said the messenger, and he ran into the open mouth of the purple purse that had toppled off the stool, spilling most of its contents. Small mirrors of all kinds lay scattered on the floor, as well as flat wooden spoons and empty dixie cups and wadded tissues and … Olivier's hockey puck.

He stooped to retrieve it, while Linnet grabbed the purse and snapped it shut, and then they tore out of the cottage before Mrs. Kidd could get to her feet again.

"Children, *darling* children, come back. Don't run away, it was only a game … don't leave, *dear* little children …"

"You're free!" Peely leapt out from behind the old apple tree to join them, and together they all ran toward the road. As Linnet clutched the purple purse to her, she could hear the little guy inside it, snapping his fingers and grumbling, "Same old story, man, kill the messenger, not cool, I shoulda bin a dentist, like my old man said, a one and a two, doo-wah, doo-wah."

Ten

They hurried along the road, unable to shake the feeling that Mrs. Kidd was following them. Peely kept glancing apprehensively behind, although the only thing in pursuit was the smoke, rolling along like a gauzy tumbleweed. Gradually they slowed down and began to breathe easier. Olivier noticed how the land was changing as they travelled farther north (north being the only way to go, in any event). It was becoming more barren and rocky, and the trees were shorter and scrubbier. It was a lot colder, too. Frost glistened on the tufts of grass along the side of the road, and the puddles in the ditch were frozen over with thin sheets of ice, the kind that on a normal day he would stop to walk on. He liked the crisp, snapping sounds the ice made when he broke through it. Thinking of this reminded him of that spoiled snob, Lord Nose, hurling bowls at the wall during dinner, smashing them to pieces. He wondered how Gramps and Sylvia and the Poets were getting on with those obnoxious guests at Cat's Eye Corner, and as he was wondering this, something odd occurred.

A small, square building appeared up ahead. It just seemed to materialize in the middle of the road, and Olivier thought it was a mirage he was seeing until Linnet said, "What's *that*? Looks like a little house, or a shed or something."

"You can see it too? Good, but if it's real, what's it doing in the middle of the road?"

"It's got to be *her*," said Peely. "That Mrs. Kidd. She's cooked up some trap, don't go near it."

"Maybe, but … that door, I recognize it." Olivier walked nearer and saw that the outside of the building was decorated with wallpaper and framed pictures. On closer inspection, the pictures turned out to be mounted jigsaw puzzles featuring the usual subjects — mountain scenery and hot air balloons and ships sailing on rough seas — but these particular ones he also recognized. That's because Gramps had done them. He loved to work on jigsaw puzzles, no matter how deadly dull the scene or how many hundreds of blue sky and cloud pieces he had to fit together. Olivier had even helped him work on some of these ones. "How about that," he said, with a little laugh. "It's the kitchen."

"What kitchen?" asked Linnet.

"From Cat's Eye Corner. I'll bet you anything that's what we'll see if we open the door. The kitchen does sometimes go missing, you know, and, well, here it is. Strange."

"I'll say. Why don't you open the door and see if you're right?"

"Don't," warned Peely. "*Don't* do it."

Olivier couldn't resist. He grabbed the doorknob and gave it a twist, and the door swung open as it always did — at least it did on the mornings he could *find* the kitchen. He peeked in and saw that everything was in its usual place — the toaster on the counter, the teakettle on the stove, the fridge with its Medusa and griffon fridge magnets on the door, the grinning cat clock on the wall (its eyes moved back and forth as the clock ticked, and it meowed on the hour) and the table in the centre of the room, upon which there appeared to be a letter with a big bite taken out of it. *That's from my parents,* he thought. He ran in and snatched it up, but on opening it saw that it was only a caterer's bill for a long list of unusual and expensive sound-ing dishes: caviar pizza, truffle burgers, pickled silverfish on toast, roast peasant (a spelling error?!), fresh hundred-dollar bills lightly sautéed and served on a bed of rare orchids. The sum for this extravagant fare was missing because of the bite, but it had to be enormous. Sylvia's posh guests were going to ruin her.

"Too rich for me," said Linnet, who had come in behind him and was reading the bill. "D'you think we can find some real food here?" She set the purple purse on the table and unsnapped the clasp. "He's awfully quiet in there. Hope he's okay." She stared down into the bottom of the purse and saw that the messenger was curled up underneath a hankie, his head resting on a peppermint (which couldn't have been too comfortable). "He must be asleep."

"I doubt it, I mean about the food. My step-step-step-gramma's not much of a cook. Not of anything you'd want to eat. Peely, come on in, it's only the kitchen."

"No thanks." He was hovering outside the door.

"Keep watch, then. Don't let the door close whatever you do." Olivier wandered over to the kitchen window and looked out. What he saw outside was the garden at Cat's Eye Corner, and not the barren landscape that they were travelling through. "Maybe we shouldn't be in here, Linnet. What if the kitchen decides to return to the house … and we go with it, right back to the beginning and no closer to finding Murray?"

"Crumb, I hadn't thought of that. Too bad, 'cause it's nice and warm in here, and we could make some tea. Are you sure there's nothing to eat? Something we could take with us?"

Olivier went over to the fridge and pulled it open. "Ice cream," he shuddered. "A flavour called Gold Chip." Someone had left the carton open on the shelf, and he closed it and put it back in the freezer. "There's a plate of sandwiches here. Little crustless ones." He picked one up and opened it. "Cucumber, and some kind of leaves."

"Watercress," said Linnet. "I've had those at Fathoms' place. They'll do, let's take them."

Olivier began filling his pockets with the sandwiches, thinking of Fathom, another friend he'd made on his last adventure, and of Fathom's watery home in the river. "Linnet —" He was going to ask her about him, and tell her about his dream, too, and how Sylvan had appeared in it, when he heard a scuffling noise outside, followed by a sudden BANG as the door slammed shut.

"Whoops." Linnet rushed over to it and tried to turn the knob, twisting and rattling it. "Guess what? It's locked.

We're trapped, twice in one day!"

Olivier shut the fridge and hurried over to try the door himself. It wouldn't budge. "Peely, are you all right?" he shouted through the door. "What's happening out there? Can you open it from your side?"

No answer.

They both stood staring at it, listening intently. In the distance they could hear some disturbing sounds.

"What's that crashing noise?"

"Is that someone screaming?"

"I could have sworn I heard a cat yowling. Don't tell me we *are* back at Cat's Eye Corner," groaned Olivier.

"Hepcats, yeah."

"You're awake," said Linnet, turning to look at the messenger, who had climbed out of the purse and was balancing on its lip.

"Hey, baby," he said, hopping onto the table and adjusting his sunglasses.

"Hi there," said Linnet. She introduced herself and Olivier, who walked over to the table to meet him.

"Name's Jack. Lay some skin on me, man."

"Skin?" Olivier made a face.

"Yeah. Can you dig it?" The little guy held out his hand.

This apparently was some kind of hand-shaking ritual. Olivier wondered if Jack was a Shriner or a member of some secret society. Then he remembered something he'd read in his book of everything. Laying a pinkie on Jack's outstretched hand, he said eagerly, "Nice to meet you, I mean, it sure is groovy. Far out. *Heavy*. Bet it's not your bag, eh, being so short? Uh, got a *hang-up* about that?"

Now it was Jack's turn to make a face. "Don't wig out on me, man."

"You mean you're not a hippie?" Olivier was disappointed, having read all about these interesting beings from another era, but he had to admit that the identifying field marks weren't right. Jack's hair was too short and the clothes too dark, and he wasn't wearing any beads or flowers.

"Hey, I'm *hip*, baby." Jack began snapping his fingers. "'Cause I'm the jazz messenger, doo-wah, doo-wah. Dig?"

"I think, I, ahh … dig." Olivier was starting to get the hang of this lingo.

"So, like, how come I'm as big as a fork, man?"

Olivier explained about the remote and what had been happening at Mrs. Kidd's cottage when Jack arrived.

"What a drag." Jack looked himself over. "My shades, my threads … crazy. Better put 'er in reverse, daddy-o."

"Reverse?"

"That's it!" said Linnet. Still standing by the door, ear pressed against it and listening for any telltale noises, she distinctly heard someone pass by outside, muttering, *Pearls, my pearls, I can't find them anywhere.*

"What is it? Is Peely in trouble?"

"I don't think Peely's out there," said Linnet. "That is, we're not there. But one of the buttons on the remote will take us back. There's got to be one that reverses what the others do."

"A kind of rewind function, you mean? Might be, but which one? It's pretty dangerous testing them out, you know."

"Sure, but we already know what four of them do. The ruby explodes things …"

"The emerald is for fast forward, the opal stops things, or freezes them."

"The topaz shrinks 'em, baby."

Olivier took the remote out of his pocket and studied it. "That leaves the sapphire button, the diamond and the pearl."

"The pearl," said Linnet. "Try that one. I don't know where the kitchen has taken us, but I heard someone outside saying something about pearls. Could have been a clue, a message for us."

"What if that someone was Mrs. Kidd?"

"Good point. Um, okay, aim it at the toaster and see what happens."

"Done." Olivier pointed the remote at the toaster and pressed the pearl button. Immediately the toaster started to bubble and snap and smoke. The metal softened and began to sag, and in a matter of seconds the whole thing had melted into a silvery pool that lay hissing and steaming on the counter.

"Like wow, man," said Jack. "*Cool.*"

"Not so cool if I'd aimed it at you."

"We could melt the door," offered Linnet. "Or blow it up same as you did before."

"I've already fried Sylvia's toaster, I shouldn't wreck her door, too. What if Gramps is standing behind it, or one of the Poets? Wait, I'm going to try another button. I don't know why, but I have a feeling this may be the one we need." Olivier aimed the remote again, this time at the cat clock, and clicked the sapphire button.

It stopped ticking, the cat's eyes widened for a moment as if in alarm (even though it wasn't *that* kind of clock), then the second hand began to whirl in the opposite direction — counterclockwise — as did the minute hand. The hour hand, which had been moving toward two o'clock, likewise began to creep back until it reached the figure 1, where it stopped. *Meeoww!* announced the clock, sounding both surprised and annoyed at having done so.

"Let's see," said Linnet. "If it's earlier, time-wise, we should be back." She tried the knob again and the door opened easily.

"Oh, man! Let's beat it." Jack jumped onto the slat of a kitchen chair, shimmied down and ran though the open doorway.

"Olivier, what are you waiting for?" Linnet herself was halfway out.

Hesitant, and still eyeing at the clock, he said, "What if we've gone too far back in time, and when we go out, we see ourselves coming down the road?"

"Then we'll have a party! Let's go."

"Sounds good to me." He followed behind her as she ran outside.

As it turned out, they didn't need to worry about encountering themselves on the road. Besides the smoke, which had formed itself into a wispy bongo drum, only Peely was waiting there. Jack had been stopped in his tracks by the sight of the ghost.

"That didn't take long," Peely said, perplexed. "No time at all. Guess you didn't find anything, eh? Wait'll I tell you, though, the strangest thing happened. It was sort of like a dream. I could see myself struggling with what's-her-name, that Vivid lady, she was *here* and I was trying to stop her from going inside, then the door slammed shut and the whole kitchen just vanished. But … none of that happened, because here you are, and she's not."

"Man oh man, a real gone guy."

"We'd better get moving," said Olivier. "It did happen, Peely, or it *will* if we don't scram. Last thing we need is to run into *her* again. I'll explain as we go."

"Dude, how about it? Lay some of those crazy rays on me."

"You mean … oh, right." Olivier pointed the remote at Jack, but couldn't bring himself to press the sapphire button. It had worked well enough with the clock and the kitchen, but what if zapping him didn't restore him to his usual size? Only made him a lot younger, or did something else entirely? "Are you sure?"

"Fire away, daddy-o. Gotta split, got some messages to deliver, doo-wah doo-wah."

Olivier closed his eyes, crossed the fingers on his other hand for luck, and pressed the button.

"It worked!" said Peely.

"*Whew*." Olivier opened his eyes again and saw that the messenger was back to normal. Jack was nodding his head, snapping his fingers and smiling as he looked himself over.

"Man, you're the *end*," he said to Olivier.

"I'm glad you're not. Ended, that is."

"Yeah," said Linnet. (Although, frankly, she preferred him tiny — it was like having a grown-up for a pet.) "You can't come with us?"

"No way, baby. Hafta make some bread."

"I have bread," said Olivier, and pulled one of the crustless sandwiches out of his pocket and offered it to Jack.

"You cats are *too much*," he laughed. "No thanks, man. But I've got a message to lay on you. There's a real square up ahead, you gotta get round, and there's this crazy little chick, she'll help you make tracks across the river. Stay cool, hang loose, don't get bent outta shape. I'm gonna split, doo-wah doo-wah, catch ya later."

The jazz messenger then shuffled off down the road, leaving them not much enlightened about what exactly lay ahead.

"A square, and round, and bent? Sounds more like geometry," said Peely. "And some *chicken* is going to help us?"

Olivier shrugged. "We won't have any trouble staying cool, I can tell you that much. We better move it." He took a bite out of his sandwich and offered a handful of them to Linnet and to Peely, who declined as usual. They resumed their northward journey, talking as they went, filling Peely in on what had happened in the kitchen, and in turn he told them about sneaking around outside of Mrs. Kidd's cottage, trying to figure out a way to rescue them. The mention of her made Linnet realize that she'd left the purple purse behind, and they speculated what would happen to it when the kitchen arrived back at Cat's Eye Corner. They also wondered why so many mirrors had come spilling out of the purse when it fell off the stool, but that puzzle stumped them. Surely a person needed only one mirror, even a person as vain and selfish as Mrs. Kidd?

Eventually they came to another fork in the road and a sign that indicated the way to the Ice Cream Palace. According to this sign, both roads led to the Palace but one was a much shorter distance than the other. Three longueurs as opposed to a fifty-two and a half! Taking the shorter route was very appealing, as they were all shivering with the cold and anxious to finally get to this place. Yet they remembered Uncle Truckbuncle's advice about taking the more roundabout way, and this had to be it. Reluctantly but determinedly they veered to the left, climbing up a rocky track that soon dwindled into a path that led upward into a scrubby, mountainous country. They walked and climbed and walked some more — and if that wasn't tiresome enough, they soon discovered what Jack had meant by a "real square" — and it was a most unfortunate discovery at that.

Eleven

As they scrambled over lichen-splattered rocks and tramped over terrain that was crunchy underfoot, like dry breakfast cereal, and made their way past stunted pine trees and firs, Olivier began to regret their decision to take the longer course. He supposed that Uncle Truckbuncle had wanted them to sidestep whatever dangers lay in wait on the shorter route to the Palace, but there was something dangerously gloomy about the atmosphere up here. The higher they went, the lower he felt. He couldn't understand it, because he usually loved hiking, and this place wasn't all that different from some of the wilderness country he had explored with his parents on other summer vacations. Except it *was* different. This mountain air wasn't fresh and exhilarating, but stale and kind of smelly, like a lunch long forgotten in the bottom of your knapsack. The sky was a November grey and the air thin, and much colder the higher they climbed. They passed cataracts of water that were frozen in mid-tumble down the rocks, and here and there, drifts of snow. Nor was there much wildlife in evidence. What there was, though, definitely was different. At one point a peculiar looking bird flew past — *backwards*. It looked like a jay, but its feathers were white, pink and brown, and patterned in stripes like Neopolitan ice cream. As it zimmed by overhead, it screeched, *meeeee, meeeee, meeeee*. They also passed a mangy squirrel that was sitting on a tree stump, its patchy fur an electric blue, freezie-colour. It wasn't the least bit frightened, but glared at them and chattered angrily, then began to throw pine cones and nuts at them.

"Hey, stop it," Olivier said to the squirrel, as an acorn bounced off his head. "You shouldn't be throwing away your food supply."

This piece of sensible advice only made the animal livid, and it began to chatter even louder and tear at its fur and run in circles on the stump.

"Rabid," muttered Linnet, and they moved quickly away from the creature. "Speaking of food supply …" she added, once they'd walked a bit farther. The sandwiches Olivier had taken from the fridge were long gone.

"I'm more thirsty than hungry," said Olivier. "This water is clear enough, don't you think? We're lucky it's not frozen solid."

They had come to a stream that was tumbling and burbling over the rocks as it flowed freely down the mountainside. There was even a faint haze of what appeared to be steam rising off it. Taking a much closer look, they saw that not only was it clear, but also that it was completely devoid of life. There wasn't a single water beetle in it, or a snail, or a speck of duckweed, or even a glob of muck.

"I wouldn't try it," said Peely.

"No, I guess not." Olivier managed to refrain from saying that Peely didn't *need* water, and that he'd be too cowardly to try it anyway. This wasn't a very generous thought, he realized, but that's all there seemed to be room for in his head at the moment.

Linnet sighed loudly and a gust of air hurried away from her, then hurried right back, as if even the wind found this place inhospitable. The smoke, too, seemed to be drifting along aimlessly and low to the ground, not even bothering to form itself into different shapes and figures as it usually did.

"You think we're going in the right direction?" said Linnet. "I'd hate to be lost up here, it's depressing. I've never felt so unenergetic in my life. I can hardly lift my feet to walk any more." To demonstrate, she lifted her foot with effort, as if her shoe were made of lead, and stepped on a patch of dried moss that lay ahead on what had become a very faint path. Her demonstration took her *much* farther than expected, though. She sank right up to her knee in the moss. *Then*, with a shriek, she disappeared entirely.

"Linnet!" Olivier ran to the spot, now a hole about the size of a garbage can lid, and gazed into it. He couldn't see a thing. "Are you okay? How far down are you?"

There was no response, only a kind of murmuring noise that sounded like a television someone had left on in a distant room.

Peely, beside him, was shuffling his feet anxiously and also peering down. "Good thing it was her," he said.

"*Nice*, Peely."

"She'd be able to break her fall, with that wind power she has. She's probably not hurt or anything."

"Oh, right. I see what you mean. What's that sound, though? Why doesn't she answer?"

"Wait, I hear her, I think. Listen."

Olivier moved as close as he dared to the edge of the hole, cocked his ear and concentrated on the sound coming from below. All he could hear was that ongoing murmur, like some announcer giving a long, boring weather report, although he couldn't actually make out what was being said. Then he *did* hear her. It had to be her, another voice that came only intermittently, a polite word or two dropped like pebbles into a flowing, ceaseless stream.

The boys looked at one another, completely puzzled. Someone else was down there? Someone maybe who had also stumbled into the hole, and now this person and Linnet were having a friendly chat?

"You don't suppose it's the Vivid kook, do you?" said Peely.

The voice was monotonous enough to be hers, but no, Olivier shook his head. He didn't see how she could possibly have gotten here before them. The more important question was how to get Linnet out. One thing, it wasn't a shallow sinkhole — she had fallen a very long way down. He considered trying the remote, but wasn't exactly sure how to use it for this predicament. The sapphire button again? That might bring Linnet back to where she had been before she stepped on the hole's mossy cover, or who knows? It gave him a queasy feeling, messing around with time. On the other hand, Linnet had the power to rescue herself. She could lift herself back up in a vortex of wind, something he'd seen her do before … so why didn't she do it now?

As if trying to work out this very problem itself, the puff of smoke had been hovering overtop of the hole, all its grey matter gathered into the shape of a brain. A very wrinkled and active brain too, for it was shooting off smoky question marks in all directions, as well as lightning bolts and a few $e=mc^2$s. Finally, it must have come up with a solution, as it then formed itself into an arm with bulging biceps, which it flexed impressively a couple of times before it flew down the hole — Supersmoke to the rescue!

The boys waited to see if this had any effect at all, but it didn't seem to. The murmuring sound continued, with Linnet's voice occasionally joining in. Nor did the smoke return to give them any visual clue as to what might be happening down below.

"Linnet!" Olivier called again. "Can you hear me? What's going on?"

Still no answer.

"We have to do *something*," he said.

"Maybe we can find a rope or a vine or — *whoa*." Before he could finish, Peely *did* do something: he flew up into the air like a leaf (an autumn leaf, as he was still faintly orange). "Help, what's happening?!" Suspended off the ground, he began pedalling his feet like crazy and waving his arms frantically. He was then moved around, this way and that, until he was positioned directly over the top of the hole, and dropped … straight down. "Ahhhhhhhhhhh!" he yelled, the sound of his voice fading into silence as he fell.

Olivier leapt back and turned to run, but it was no use. He was next. He felt himself being snatched up and floated over to the opening in the ground. It was the eeriest sensation. If he had had a moment to reflect, he might have wondered if this was Linnet's doing and tried not to fight it, but he acted purely on instinct, struggling and kicking, punching at the air, desperate to free himself from this overpowering force he couldn't even see.

The next thing he knew, he was hurtling downward, feet first, along a tunnel that was carved out of rock. Down, down he went, certain that when he reached the bottom he would be smashed to pieces — there wouldn't be an unbroken bone left in his body. He closed his eyes, thinking that he'd never open them again. And then he opened them again. He had begun to slow down. Instead of zooming along at breakneck speed, he was making a more gradual descent. This sensation was equally strange, dreamlike even, but not unpleasant, as if he were skateboarding downward on a feather. He reached out to touch the side of the tunnel and found it to be slightly rough and chalky. Limestone, he thought. He looked down at his feet and saw something red and furry-looking not far below. A second later he was standing on it, an incredibly ugly shag carpet. He had floated down out of the tunnel and landed on his feet lightly, as if he had done nothing more than leap gracefully off a short step.

Olivier saw that he was in a huge cave, complete with stalagmites and stalactites, drips of water falling from the ceiling, and the sound of an underground river running nearby. Curiously, it was also a cave that was done up as a living room. Besides the shag carpet (he was standing on one edge of it), a central area was furnished with a Naugahyde couch, a brown tweed La-Z-Boy chair, a lamp with a goofy shade, a wobbly coffee table, framed photographs every-where — even a few hanging crookedly on the stalagmites — and a fireplace with fake logs glowing in it.

The smoke, no longer shaped like a well-muscled arm, was drifting around this fake fire as if trying to commu-nicate with it, and not having much luck. Linnet and Peely were both sitting on the couch, staring transfixed at a person who was holding court in the La-Z-Boy. At least Olivier *thought* it was a person, for he had a man's body, but a head that was more moose-like than man-like. He had a furry face and a long muzzle with a goatee hanging beneath it, and fair-sized antlers protruding from the sides of his head. The antlers were adorned with various objects. A dangling tea bag, as well as a monocle, a glit-tering silver ball that looked like a Christmas decoration, an air freshener, a yo-yo and a watch on a chain. This sin-gular figure was quite nattily dressed, as if he were going to a party. He had on a dinner jacket (unlike the jackets in the Odditorium, this wasn't literally a "dinner" jacket, and you couldn't eat it, but it was appealing just the same), a silk scarf tossed dashingly around his neck, mid-night blue slacks and black patent leather shoes with tassels on them. In one hand he was holding an empty martini glass and in the other a dainty cracker with a smear of green paste on it. And he was talking, on and on and on.

With effort, Linnet looked away from the prattling figure for a second and motioned Olivier over to the couch. As she did so, he felt a burly gust of wind ruffle his hair and slide off his shoulders, confirming what he should have guessed right from the start, that Linnet had used her powers to bring him down to this cave. She must have discovered something important here, he decided. It could be that this peculiar moose-man had some crucial information to impart, perhaps something that would lead them to Murray. He walked over and leaned against the arm of the couch, crossed his arms and prepared to listen.

The fellow inclined his head by way of a greeting, which made the objects dangling from his antlers rattle and clink, but he didn't stop talking. Both of Olivier's friends were utterly captivated, although he didn't find the subject of this monologue all that interesting. A bit funny, maybe. The man was telling them about something called "No Theatre."

"So the first actor declaims, 'Not to be or *not* to be.'"

"The other actor answers, 'That's *not* the question.'"

"Then the first replies, 'No?'"

"The second responds, 'No way.'"

"First, 'Never?'"

"Second, 'Not on your life.'"

"First, 'No kidding!'"

"Quite the no-show, and I could go on (and on) but I'm sure you have the idea, this kind of drama *is* rather negative, I admit, and there's no point to it really, but there's also no admission charge, did I ever tell you about the time …"

Ah, Olivier understood, he's one of those people (if he *was* a person) who like the sound of their own voices. He had an uncle like that, who was never at a loss for words, and once he got started talking he couldn't seem to stop. Every story he told had some connection to other stories, like fishing line all snarled and tangled up in a ball. Olivier usually tuned his uncle out after a while, politely smiling and nodding while thinking his own thoughts, but this fellow here wasn't just a windbag (which Linnet might not mind at any rate). If he liked the sound of his own voice … well, Olivier did, too, he realized with some surprise. You know, he thought, there *is* something extremely pleasant about it, musical almost, and soothing. As he listened, he felt himself sliding down the arm of the couch, and then he leaned up against it as he settled on the carpet.

The talker had moved on to the topic of food and drink, and he was describing a ten-course meal at length and in succulent detail. Already famished, Olivier would normally have been driven bonkers by having to hear about all this fabulous fare, but the odd thing was that by the time the guy got to the dessert course — "marmalade chocolate cake decorated with crystallized roses and violets" — he thought he might burst, he felt so full. (Olivier had heard of people eating their *own* words, but never eating anyone else's, and never words that were so satisfying.) Fortunately, the subject changed before everyone started groaning with indigestion, and their host finally got around to telling them who he was and *what* he was.

"… name's Noel, I'm a Schmooze, don't you know, and all the photographs you see about you in my humble abode are my brothers and sisters, there's Bill over there on the table, he's a Schnozz, as you can see, and then there's Dot, she's a Schlump, but she means well, and Clay, dear dear, he's a Schmuck, no doubt about it, and the one who is fast asleep in that picture on the coffee table is my cousin Noddy, a Schnorrer, he's with his famous actor friend from the great Schmaltz family, and the picture on the stalagmite, why those are our darling little dogs, the Schmutz …"

Olivier chuckled. He felt good. Terrific, even. So relaxed and cheerful, he could sit here contentedly for years. He glanced over at his friends, who were leaning up against one another, listening dreamily to Noel and smiling. What a relief it was to have that oppressive gloom they'd all felt above on the mountainside lifted from their minds. It wasn't so much what the Schmooze said as how he said it — there was something magical about his voice. What a charming fellow, Olivier thought.

"Boy, I'm dead." Peely gave a little laugh.

"Me, too," said Linnet. "Although I feel more rested now. In fact, I feel wonderful."

"No, I mean I'm dead," answered Peely. "Really. I'm a ghost."

"Neat," said Linnet. "We thought you were. Is it fun?"

"Oh yeah. Loads. You don't have to brush your teeth. You don't even have to eat."

"Wait a minute," said Olivier, struggling to speak. It seemed that all his mouth wanted to do was smile blissfully, and it's hard to speak when you're busy grinning like an idiot. "What do you mean? You said you weren't."

"Couldn't face it, I guess. I don't care now, I'd rather be a ghost. Living is so stupid and boring. There's no point, why bother."

"Hmm, maybe you're right," murmured Linnet happily.

Olivier wanted to agree, but something about this sentiment troubled him. "How do you know that you're a ghost, Peely? For sure, I mean?"

"When I was in your room, remember, and looked through that window in your book, I saw myself in there, on my bed, looking like I was a real goner. My grandmother was sitting by the bed holding my hand, and she was crying and everything, so I figured that was that. Who cares? Good to get it over with."

At this, Olivier stopped smiling and the Schmooze cranked up the volume, speaking a just a bit louder. He stretched out the hand holding the martini glass, and water that was dripping from the ceiling began slowly to fill it up — *drip, drip, drip*. The objects dangling from his antlers swayed back and forth, back and forth. Olivier felt a wave of utter indifference wash over him. Still, he managed to say, "Where were your parents?"

"Away, busy. You know how it is? Can't blame them, who'd want to take care of a sick kid? Cut your losses, my dad always says."

Some parents. Olivier *didn't* know how it was, thank goodness, and thinking of his own folks his head began to clear, and he didn't feel quite so pleased with everything. "Why *did* they call you Peely, anyway?" Not a name he'd want to be stuck with.

"That's just a nickname. What my gramma calls me, it's a joke between us. She's Scottish, you see, and in her country 'peely wally' means 'pale.' My real name is Wallace Peele."

"Wallace Peele," Olivier repeated. "I've heard that name before. *Where*, though?"

Before Olivier could think further about this — and it *was* hard to think, his brain was so fogged up — his eyes started to water. Wiping away the tears, he saw that the smoke had formed itself into a hand shape again and was poking him in the eyes, Three Stooges style, making a *V* out of its index and forefinger. "Smoke? What's up, what're you doing?" Olivier brushed it away but it only reformed itself into a pair of gauzy earmuffs, which it clamped over his ears. Then, with a leftover wisp of itself, it tickled Olivier's nose until he started to sneeze and cough, which had the desired effect.

The Schmooze suddenly stopped talking and stared at Olivier, a tad annoyed at having been so rudely interrupted. He took a tiny nibble from his cracker and a sip from his martini glass, cleared his throat and then resumed speaking again, but by this time it was too late. The spell he had been weaving was broken, and the children all blinked their eyes and looked around as if seeing the place for the first time.

"Ew," Linnet said, jumping up. "Naugahyde. Gross."

Olivier also leapt up. "Let's get out of here. Peely, get up, don't listen to him!"

"What was I saying just now?"

"Nothing, forget it," said Olivier. "This way, come on, follow the smoke."

"Yeah," said Linnet, "and let's make it *schnappy*."

The smoke had formed itself into an exit sign and was hovering at the mouth of a tunnel, beyond which they could hear the sound of the underground river. All three ran in that direction, following its lead (it *was* Supersmoke, after all). The Schmooze didn't lift a finger to stop them, but merely kept on chatting in his glib and diverting manner, and taking enormous pleasure in his own company.

Twelve

Making their way down the tunnel was not as difficult as they had expected, for it was illuminated with an eerie green light that grew stronger the farther along they went. The difficult part had more to do with wondering where they were going to end up. As he ran along it, Olivier tried not to think of tremors and cave-ins. He stayed alert to the sound of the river, which was getting louder, hoping all the while that it would lead them outside of the mountain. There had to be some sort of bank they could walk along.

This hope was dashed to smithereens when they arrived in a huge cavern through which the river was flowing. They found themselves standing on a narrow ledge, staring at a river that was alarmingly wide. There were insurmountable walls of rock on either side, and no bank at all to walk along. They'd have to jump into the river itself if they intended to follow it, and it didn't look overly inviting.

It must have been connected to that same stream they'd seen above, for it was as empty of life as a river of bleach. The green light they had followed in the tunnel seemed to be emanating from it, as were drifting swaths of steam — the cavern was as hot as a sauna. When Olivier picked up a pebble and dropped it in the water, it dissolved like a tablet.

Linnet winced. "What are we going to do now? I'd hate to go back. I never knew chit-chat could be so deadly."

"We're done for," groaned Peely.

"Not yet. Look over there, someone's coming. In a rowboat." Olivier was pointing upstream, where indeed a small black vessel had appeared out of the dark. It was moving toward them, oars dipping silently into the water. Soon the boat was gliding nearer and they were able to see who was rowing it: — a young girl with a dirty face and ratty black hair, wearing jeans and an overlarge shirt that were ripped and smudged. She had on a pair of bashed-up work boots (although they couldn't quite see that) and oven mitts on her hands. The boat was made of metal, as were the oars, and would conduct the heat of the river, Olivier realized. She needed the mitts for protection. When the boat pulled up alongside them, he saw that the seats were outfitted with thick, quilted chair pads, similar to the kind in his parents' kitchen.

"Right," she said, "hop in. That'll be a mirror each." She then looked at Peely, narrowing her eyes. The puff of smoke was suspended above his head like an empty thought balloon. "No charge for you. Looks like you're paid up already."

"What do you mean 'mirrors'? *Who* are you, anyway?" asked Linnet.

"I'm Sharon. I'll ferry you across this river, the Stynx. You won't get across any other way. There's Shuks guarding the bridge and they only let in the tour buses and the prisoners. Mirrors are the currency here, don't you know that?"

"All those mirrors in Mrs. Kidd's purse," said Olivier.

"Shoot. I would've grabbed some, if I'd known," said Linnet. "Is there anything else you'll accept?" Not that she had anything to offer. "How about that puck thing, Olivier?"

He didn't want to give *that* away (you never knew when a sudden game of road hockey might break out), but what else were they going to do? The remote wasn't a possibility. So he drew the puck out of his pocket and offered it to Sharon. She only made a face and said, "Don't you have anything else?"

He dug even deeper in his pocket, felt something in amongst the lint and sandwich crumbs, and pulled it out — a gold coin. "Hmph, what's this doing here?"

"The *doit*," said Linnet.

"I don't remember putting it in my pocket. It was in my room with all my other stuff." The doit was a souvenir from Olivier's last adventure, during which it had come in very handy. Maybe it would now, too. He handed it to Sharon, saying, "Will this do?"

"I'd rather have silver, but let's have a look." Removing one oven mitt, she took the doit and examined it, grinning when she saw the huge nose that was embossed on the one side. "Reminds me of the Empress. She's got a real beak —

a total honker. Okay, hop in, I'll take you." She slipped the coin in the pocket of her jeans. "If you got past Mrs. Kidd's place, you deserve a ride, anyway."

"I'm not getting in that boat," Peely spoke up. "You don't have any life preservers. I don't see a single one."

"I wouldn't worry about it if I were you," she said.

"I don't see the chicken. It was supposed to help us across — Jack, that messenger guy said."

"Well, *I* see it," she laughed. "In, everybody! Move it, we're wasting time."

Olivier and Linnet climbed into the boat right away and Peely followed reluctantly. Olivier claimed the bow while the other two settled in the stern. Sharon pushed off from the ledge with one of the oars, sat back down on the middle seat — the thwart — and began rowing.

Olivier studied the rocky sides of the cavern as they moved past and looked down into the water. Unnatural how empty the river was. Normally he would have trailed his fingers in it, but he knew better than to do that here, considering what had happened to that pebble he'd dropped in and to his shirt, too, when a drop of water flew off Sharon's oar and landed on it. The water burned a hole right through the cloth. Good thing the river itself was moving along sluggishly. It would be dicey if they hit some rapids, and he couldn't help but worry a little about that rumbling noise he heard in the distance. When he asked Sharon about it, she told him that it was only the ice cream factory he was hearing.

"Goes night and day, never stops," she said.

"I thought it was a palace?" said Linnet.

"That's where the nobs live, but the factory pays for it all. It's behind the palace, you'll see. Why're you going there, anyway? You wanna steal some ice cream? Other kids have tried, you know, and no one's ever done it."

"We're going to rescue a friend," said Olivier.

"Lots have tried that too ... and never been seen again."

At this, Peely made a small whimpering sound, but Olivier asked, "Why? What happens to them?"

"Dunno," Sharon said.

"Anything you can tell us at all might be helpful," Olivier persisted.

"All I know is that kids go into that place, the factory, and don't come out again. Never go anywhere near it myself, and no one's been able to catch me on the river here. You guys shouldn't, either. There's a spot I can let you off downstream, and you can scram, go back the way you came."

"Okay," said Peely.

"*Non possumus,*" said Linnet, referring to the Latin inscription on the other side of the doit.

"Exactly. It's *not* possible," Olivier agreed wholeheartedly. "We're not backing out now."

Sharon nodded and rowed onward, steadily, through the dim greenish light, and it wasn't long after that they emerged from the mountainside through an opening at its base. Here the Stynx grew even wider as several tributaries fed into it, and she ferried them along expertly without anyone getting splashed with the vile water.

The first thing they saw rising in the distance on the other side was the Ice Cream Palace. They couldn't help but see it, because the building was so incredibly gaudy. It featured several domes that were shaped like huge soft ice cream scoops, and these were all brightly coloured — lemon yellow, grape, bubble gum pink, chocolate swirl, tiger tail. The Palace was decorated as well with minarets and towers, weather vanes and flags, and shiny objects stuck in the walls that looked like enormous sprinkles. On the whole it had the appearance of being *made* of ice cream, although that didn't seem possible.

"Holy doodle!" said Peely, which just about summed up what Linnet and Olivier were thinking.

Downstream they saw a bridge fording the river, with a guardhouse at one end and several Shuks standing around. A tour bus was idling on the bridge and the stone men were busy collecting tickets from the passengers and checking the bus to make sure all was in order.

"Timed it perfectly," Sharon said quietly. "There's been some trouble brewing lately, so the Shuks aren't taking any chances with who they let onto the Palace grounds. They're not even looking this way, I'll row you straight across. I can land where that dead grass is. It's tall enough to hide you if you crouch down."

"What kind of trouble?" asked Olivier.

"Some rebel parents I've heard. They're planning something, I don't know what, but I'm gonna help whatever it is."

"Good," he said, smiling at her. "So will we."

"Here you are, then." She slid the rowboat into some tall dried reeds by the riverbank. As the bow nudged closer to land, Olivier jumped out, then held onto the painter while the others moved forward. "Good luck," she said, once everyone was out. She pushed the boat away from the bank with an oar. "Watch out for the dog."

"Dog?"

"ViceVersa," she called, now in midstream again and rowing away. "It's got two heads. One of them is friendly enough, but the other is *vicious*." She waved goodbye.

"Wonderful," said Linnet. "A two-headed dog."

"I don't even like one-headed dogs," said Peely.

"I'd say there's lots of things here not to like." Olivier was observing a pipe at their feet out of which a gel-like liquid was flowing. The smell of it was terrible, like sour milk and dead worms and something chemical, and the stuff was oozing out of the pipe directly into the river. "We'd better sneak around the back and check out this factory first."

They set out through the long dry grass, crouching low, as Sharon had advised. It was a good enough cover, Olivier supposed, as long as no one was scanning the field from an upstairs window of the Palace or from one of its towers. He glanced up as they skirted around it. Quite the place! He then saw that a Shuk *was* standing guard in one of the towers, but again, luckily, the guard's attention was directed elsewhere — at the tour bus that was now headed up the drive. As the bus moved along, it was play-ing the tinkly music you sometimes hear coming from ice cream carts, and the faces of the passengers were pressed against the windows — all adults, but all beaming and as eager looking as excited five-year-olds. From Olivier's van-tage, it was hard to tell for certain, but the Shuk appeared to be watching the bus with an expression of disgust. This made Olivier wonder if he was like the one who had helped him in the amphitheatre. He wished he knew more about the Shuks and what hold it was that this Emperor had over them. He didn't think it could be doctored ice cream in their case, unless there was a flavour they just couldn't resist — rocky road, say.

Once they had advanced far enough around the side of the Palace, they saw it, the factory, and they let out a collective gasp. It was such a grim, grey place. It was a large building, squat and square, and could have easily been a prison (or a really ugly school). There were tangles of barbed wire around the outside, a bolted front door, and a single grimy window high up on the side nearest them. They could hear machinery chugging and thumping away inside, as well as someone shouting out the same phrase over and over again: "I SCREAM YOU SCREAM WE ALL SCREAM FOR ICE CREAM! I SCREAM YOU SCREAM …!"

Olivier gave a start, because he recognized this. It was part of the chorus from the "Ice Cream Song" that Gramps sometimes sang for him. The song had a bouncy tune and wacky lyrics, but here it sounded insane.

"I've got to see what's going on in there." Frowning, he gazed up at the window, which was too high for him to reach. "Think you could give me a boost, Linnet?"

"Sure thing." She swept her hands through the air a couple of times, and in a second he felt himself rising up along the wall as if supported on an invisible pair of shoulders. He grasped the small sill when he got to it, and rubbed his sleeve against the glass. Peering down at the factory floor, he saw a mass of machinery all thumping and bumping and working away. There were valves and pipes, tanks and vats, machines that dropped dixie cups onto conveyer belts, machines that filled them with ice cream and machines that fastened lids on them, then bore them away into a huge freezer. Attending all this machinery, and labouring like machines themselves, were children of all ages. Pulling levers, pushing buttons, filling vats, mixing, sorting, checking — they all had specific jobs that they repeated continuously. This was terrible enough (imagine how boring and tiring it would be!), but they also had to listen to the constant "I SCREAM YOU SCREAM" that was blaring out of a loudspeaker. Even worse, pieces of duct tape sealed their mouths, presumably so that they couldn't sample the goods — or speak to one another. In fact, it didn't look as though they got to sample much of anything in the way of food. Olivier was shocked at how thin and pale they were, and at how sad and defeated they looked. No light in their eyes, no spirit. Just work work work.

Boy, he clenched his jaw, this was criminal. He was already making plans to free those hapless kids and blow this darn factory to molecules when he felt his footing give way and heard Peely cry out.

"Help! Oh, eeh, ick, help!"

Olivier fell to the ground. It didn't hurt *too* much.

"*Sorry*," said Linnet. "I was distracted by … hey you, get away, shoo!"

Olivier jumped to his feet and ran to join Linnet, who was trying to save Peely from the attentions of a mega-mongrel with two heads. He'd come face to face to face with ViceVersa, the two-headed dog. The head that belonged to the Vice half was growling and baring its big, sharp, grotty teeth at Peely, while the other, Versa, was attempting to lick him with its long, slobbering tongue, as though *he* were made of ice cream (he *was* still an orange sherbet colour). Poor Peely. Not only was he terrified by Vice and grossed out by Versa, but he was getting a double dose of dog breath.

Olivier reached for the remote. He didn't want to hurt the dog, only scare it away, so he had to think fast. Opal? Topaz? Sapphire? Emerald? Freeze it, shrink it, turn it into a puppy, or send it scooting off on fast forward?

While he hesitated, considering his options, it was the smoke that jumped in and saved the day once again. As it had done much earlier in their adventure, it formed itself into the shape of a cat, no more substantial than a shadow. This immediately caught the dog's attention, cat pursuit evidently being one issue that the two very different heads were in agreement on. When the smoke arched its back and then shot off toward the Palace, so did the dog, in hot pursuit. Very hot, because before it did so, Vice snapped at Peely's ankle and ripped off the piece of his sock upon which a sun was glowing brightly. As the dog ran, Versa barked raucously and joyfully, while Vice's angry mouth blazed with the snagged sun, as if he were bearing away a torch.

"Are you all right?" Linnet bent down to examine Peely's foot. "Did it hurt you?" She didn't see how it could have, given Peely's ghostly condition, but there did seem to be a wound or a mark of some kind on his ankle where the sock had been torn away.

"I'm okay," he sniffed.

"Olivier, have a look at this, will you?" she said, puzzled.

But there was no time. Olivier raised his hand in warning, for beyond the racket that the factory was making, he could hear voices, grown-up ones. It was the tour heading their way.

"Quick, follow me." He indicated the back of the factory, and they all took off in that direction, Peely surging ahead of the other two despite his ankle. Olivier thought for sure there would be some junk around back that they could hide behind, but when they got there, they found something else instead. Something that was at once both fabulous and frightening.

Thirteen

"He looks like Sleeping Beauty," said Linnet. "Sleeping Handsome, I mean."

"Sleeping Adequate, anyway," said Peely, although no one laughed at his joke.

Olivier didn't know what to say, except mournfully to himself, *too late, too late*.

All three had their noses pressed against a marvellous ice sculpture. It was marvellous not only because of its intricate detail and the beauty of its craftsmanship, but because of what it represented — Cat's Eye Corner. Although only the size of a playhouse, the sculpture was an exact replica of the mansion. True, it had a different name — The Writer's Block — carved in the cornice above the front door, but Olivier saw within rooms he recognized, and furniture, and any number of familiar knick-knacks. There *was* one room in the very heart of this ice house that he'd never before encountered (which was not unusual in

the real Cat's Eye Corner, of course), and that did indeed
appear to be a block, a solid block of ice. It caught his eye
immediately because embedded in the centre of the block
was … Murray!

"Don't worry, Olivier, he'll be all right. We just have to
get him out of there," said Linnet.

"How can you be so sure?" He tried to keep his voice
steady. "He's got to be frozen solid."

"He's tough, and he's, uh, survived worse." Linnet's
face reddened at this, for *she* was the one responsible for
the last worse thing that had happened to him.

"How come this ice sculpture is like my grandmother's
house?" said Peely.

"It's not," said Olivier. "I mean it is, or *was*, because it
belongs to my step-step-stepgramma now. Your grandmother
must have moved away for some reason …" He caught
sight of Peely's stricken expression, and quickly changed
the subject. "I don't exactly know, Peely. We'll figure it out,
I promise, but right now I've got to help Murray. What do
you think? I could hit the pearl button on the remote?
That should melt the ice, but what if it melts Murray, too?
I don't think I can chance it."

"I could use some wind muscle to lift the house up,
and then drop it," said Linnet.

"Yeah, smash it," said Peely, who looked as if he wouldn't
mind seeing it destroyed.

"That might hurt Murray, too. Same thing if I use the
ruby button." Olivier tapped his foot, thinking, thinking.
He stared in at his friend, at his black barrel and cap,
which had turned a deep blue with the cold. Horrible to

imagine what he must have gone through since he was pennapped. And how did he end up here, prisoner in a frozen house, and one that was so cruelly named for someone with writerly ambitions?

"I've got it!" Linnet said. "Something that won't hurt at all. It'll be like a kiss of life. Just give me a minute, I have to concentrate. This country is so cold." She closed her eyes and began to move her lips, mumbling something that sounded like *simoom sirocco solano harmattan snoweater chinook*. She repeated this several times, the boys watching her closely.

Before long they began to feel a soft, southerly breeze flowing around them — and in Peely's case, right *through* him. Ohhh, Olivier thought, *this is so nice*. The breeze even smelled nice — of watermelon, and hot dogs, and sunscreen (if you like that smell), and the ocean. A beach ball then bounced by, and someone's straw hat sailed through the air like a spaceship and caught on a turret of the ice house.

The breeze, moving lazily at first, now picked up speed and extra heat. It circled around The Writer's Block, faster and faster, and as it did so the windows and doors began to soften and melt. It streamed into the house and whistled through it, as Olivier himself had often done in Cat's Eye Corner, running along the halls and up and down the stairs. Walls grew thin and fragile, the roof suddenly slid off and shattered on the ground, the attic folded, the third floor collapsed into the second, the chimney caved in completely. In no time at all, it seemed, the only thing left of the beautiful ice sculpture was the block with Murray suspended in it … and in a wink (several, actually) even that was gone. The breeze snatched up the straw hat, now floating in a pool of water, and drifted off with it toward the palace.

"You did it!" Olivier ran to retrieve his pen friend from the sodden ground. "Murray," he gasped. "It's me, Olivier. You're safe, we found you. Are you okay? Can you write?"

Murray was awfully cold, *deathly* cold. Olivier knew that he should give him some time to warm up and recover, but he was so anxious about him that straightaway he plucked the notebook out of his shirt pocket and poised Murray to speak — if he could.

There was a long, agonizing moment while they all waited for something to happen. Linnet and Peely were both glued motionless to the spot as they watched Murray and Olivier and the notebook. Then, haltingly, Murray began to write a few words, and then a few more, but these were very hard to read because they were frozen, his script similar to the kind that Jack Frost uses when he writes on windowpanes. *Now … is … the winter … of my … discontent!* he wrote. Then, picking up speed, *My king-dom for … a vat of … horseradish!!* He continued, moving along at quite a clip, *Rage, rage, against the dying of the fire!!!* Racing along the page now, *Some are born cold, some achieve coldness and some have coldness thrust upon them, like ME for instance!!!!* He went on in this vein for some time, rapidly filling up pages of the notebook. Olivier could hardly keep up, but he let him go on, thinking that it might be good for him to get it out of his system. Murray was really annoyed, and understandably so.

"He's kind of rattled. Seems like his old self, though," said Linnet.

"Maybe that's what happens when you get sprung from The Writer's Block," suggested Peely. "Once you're out, you can't stop writing."

"Yeah," said Olivier, his hand beginning to cramp.

Fortunately Murray's frosty and indignant tone soon started to thaw, and his words took on their normal hue as his ink warmed. *Oh, my boy, I am SO glad to see you! And Linnet, dear, and even you, Orange Peel.*

"It's *Peely*," said Peely, a bit indignant himself.

Yes, yes, of course. But listen, we can't stop here, a guard will be by soon to check on me. I can't understand why he hasn't been already. Let's ——

Murray was interrupted by an alarm bell that had started clanging in the distance. This noise was followed by someone calling out, then shouting, and then several people joined in and they were all shouting, too.

"Help," cried Peely. "We've been *caught*."

Heavens, Casper, get a grip. Some nervy child is probably trying to make a break for it.

"It's *Peely*," he grumbled.

Right you are, McDuff. Now listen everyone. We'll have to exercise extreme caution, these people mean business. After we find out what this ruckus is about, I'll lead you to a hiding place I discovered in the palace. From there we can make our plans.

"Excellent," said Olivier.

"Let's do it," said Linnet.

"*What* plans?" said Peely. "We've got you now, so let's go home. I'm not going in that palace. You guys must be crazy.

This place is dangerous, in case you haven't noticed. You're going to let a *pen* tell you what to do?" He was suddenly fed up with this whole adventure. Just plain *sick* of it. Nobody could see him for what he really was, and that dumb pen couldn't even get his name right.

Not much spirit, for a spirit, has he?

"Peely, we can't go home without helping these kids," said Olivier. "They're prisoners, and being forced to work here. It's not right. You can go, if you want."

"Fine. I *will*. Goodbye."

And much to everyone's surprise, he turned on his heel and stomped off, noiselessly, and disappeared around the corner of the factory.

"Gosh, will he be safe?" said Linnet.

"He's the safest one here."

Bah, he'll be back before I can dot my i's and cross my t's. Or is that — before I can cross my i's ...

"Ha, they didn't hurt your sense of humour, Murray."

The pun is mightier than the sword, my boy. Come, you two, let's see what all the bellowing is about. One of the tourists probably dropped his scoop of ice cream on the ground.

They retraced their steps along the side of the factory, Murray comfortably and happily riding once again in Olivier's shirt pocket. They expected to find Peely lurking there, still nursing his grievance, but there was no sign of him. More worried now, they were hoping he hadn't gotten into any trouble. Definitely wanting to keep out of trouble themselves, both Linnet and Olivier were proceeding as quietly and cautiously as they could.

When they arrived at the front of the factory, they hid

behind some barrels, fragrant with vanilla, which had been stacked there. This allowed them to see what was happening up ahead, without being seen themselves. A crowd had gathered at the back wall of the palace and were gaping at a corner tower. The crowd, composed of Shuks, people from the tour and palace servants, were *oohing* and *ahhing* as they watched large drips of molten material roll down the side of the building. The whole tower was leaning wickedly and was about to topple over at any moment.

"The palace *is* made of ice cream," he whispered to Linnet.

"Yes," she smiled. "I think that breeze I summoned wanted a little tour of the place before it blew home. Oh, look."

Linnet pointed to a Shuk. The straw hat was perched jauntily on the top of his head and he was holding the beach ball in front of him like a melon and studying it with interest.

Trumpets then began to sound, and everyone's attention was diverted to a procession of individuals who had emerged from the palace. Leading this procession were two trumpet players dressed in strawberry pink and mint green livery, and another fellow in butterscotch, who was proclaiming, "Oy yay, oy yay, let the lamp affix its beam ... make way, make way, for the Emperor (and 'er, the Empress) of Ice Cream."

When these two royal personages strode into view at an excruciatingly stately pace, Olivier's jaw dropped. He was astonished at how closely they resembled Lord Nose and Lady Muck, except they were the exact reverse. The Emperor was tall with messy, matted hair, and with ice cream stains and cigar ash all down the front of his shirt (and buttons in the wrong buttonholes). The Empress was short and tubby, with a big honker of a nose stuck straight up in the air. (Sharon was right about that!) They were both wearing tinfoil crowns and robes that looked to be made of cat fur (Olivier shuddered at this), hers tabby and his calico. The Emperor was also tightly gripping a lead that appeared to be made of red licorice and on the end of which skittered a tiny monkey. This had to be Pistachio, the very monkey who had stolen Murray. Seeing it bound in this way, though, Olivier felt sorry for the unfortunate creature. It was obviously a captive as well.

All of the tourists in the crowd were staring goggle-eyed at the Emperor and Empress, and they in turn were soaking up the admiring attention like sponges. If they had once been humble ice cream sellers, they certainly weren't that now. They were all puffed up with themselves, as Gramps would say, which the Emperor proved the moment he opened his mouth.

"You!" He snapped his fingers at one of the Shuks. "I want this tower fixed by tea time. Got that, stonehead?" He then turned to the crowd and with a nasty smile, said, "The *help* these days, you've no idea. Pebbles for brains."

The tourists all laughed uproariously at this, although the Shuk who had been insulted only stared at the Emperor (how else?) stonily.

"Almost as stupid as *children*," added the Empress, addressing the sky, it seemed.

This was met with vigorous nods of agreement and more laughter.

"Ugh, *children*," the Emperor bristled. "So immature. So sloppy and uncouth." He wiped his nose on his sleeve.

"They're *short*," she said, appalled.

"And they *whine*," he whined.

"They're unnecessary!" someone shouted from the crowd.

"Shut up, I'M speaking," barked the Emperor. "Children are *rude*, I hate that. They're *cruel*, too." He gave the lead a sharp jerk, and the ink monkey flew backward, chattering with pain and fright. "Thus, *sniff sniff*, in a brilliant and original conclusion, I'd have to say that children are … *unnecessary*."

"Ooooo," intoned the crowd. "Bravo! Long live the Emperor (and 'er, the Empress) of Ice Cream!!"

"You can bet on that, bozos, we *will* live long." The Emperor and Empress exchanged a smug little look, and then, having gratified the commoners long enough with their royal presence, they turned and proceeded slowly back toward the palace, along with their entourage.

Linnet and Olivier both groaned. The pair was almost too ridiculous to take seriously, although they knew they had to, and the sooner the better. Olivier noticed that the Shuk who had been ordered to fix the tower was doing nothing of the kind. He was still standing firmly in place, and another Shuk had come up to him and together they were conferring about something. Olivier recognized this second Shuk. It was the same one who had helped him earlier, and who later had silently warned him off doing anything rash while the child prisoners were being marched along the road. Olivier wondered if he should try to attract this Shuk's attention — surely he would help them — and was just about to seek Murray's advice when someone silently approached from behind and grabbed them roughly.

"'Ere, you two! How'd you get out, ya lazy brats? Get back in the factory, or you'll be doin' triple overtime an' no crusts for yer supper. Maybe ya wanna spend some time in the locker, eh?"

It was a foreman from the factory, ugly as a pirate, who had mistaken them for a couple of workers.

"Watch out!" Olivier shouted. "The *tower*."

Instantly the foreman let go of them, which was the whole idea, but it was no lie. The tower *was* falling, and it came down like a rocket, crashing into the ground and sending slabs of white chocolate, gobs of soft ice cream, jagged bits of candy and sugary bricks and chunks of wall flying everywhere. In the pandemonium that followed, with everyone, including the foreman, screaming and running for cover, Olivier and Linnet fled toward the palace. They slipped in through a back door that was dull-silver and heavy, but child-sized. It even had a sign on it that said CHILLDREN. Somebody goofed, thought Linnet, briefly recalling her own spelling triumph at Mrs. Kidd's. This wasn't a mistake, however, and they soon discovered why.

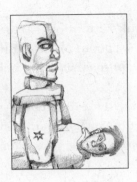

Fourteen

If there was any way that Murray could have stopped them from entering the palace through *this* particular door, he surely would have. But everything happened so fast that all he could do when he saw where they were headed in a mad rush was ink to himself, *Good grief, not again, I just thawed out!*

"Br-r-r-r," said Linnet, a second after they'd entered, her teeth chattering so hard she could barely speak. "A-a-nd I-I-I th-th-ought it-it-it was c-c-c-c-old outs-s-s-side."

Olivier started to answer, and then found he couldn't. A deep stupefying cold struck him with full force. Once again, as he'd been at Mrs. Kidd's place when she'd zapped them with the remote, he was frozen solid. Although this time the freezing felt different, and was even more unpleasant. At first, a troubling sadness swept through him, and then a feeling of complete hopelessness, and after that he didn't feel anything at all. He might as well have been a block of stone — or ice. A dead weight. All sensation was gone from his body, except for a spark of heat he noticed in the vicinity of his shirt pocket, where Murray, outraged, was fuming. This gave Olivier the idea of trying to generate some mindfire of his own, so that his brain wouldn't freeze over entirely. He had to do something to save himself ... and Linnet, but where was she?

The room was dimly lit by a source of light that he couldn't quite see, as he was only able to look straight ahead. At least he still could see, although it was more like peering through frosted windows than using his own sharp eyes.

He couldn't locate Linnet — he figured she had to be close by — but that's when he saw the children. Row upon row of them — *all frozen*. From what he could tell, there seemed to be hundreds of them lined up ahead of him. They were all ages (some only toddlers!) and were organized in rows according to size and shape, like merchandise. This room had to be the locker that the foreman had threatened to send them to for punishment ... and they had run right into it! It looked as though they stored their spare supply of factory workers here, keeping them fresh until the others wore out from overwork. He assumed that all these kids *could* be thawed out and revived. He refused to think otherwise. If *only* he could reach his remote.

Olivier was determined not to let the same thing happen to him. He knew that the intense cold here could so easily pinch out his last spark of consciousness, but he wasn't going to let it. *Think*, he ordered himself, *come on, anything*. He recited the names of the provinces to himself, *and* their capitals, then the names of all the prime ministers, then all the different kinds of butterflies he could think of — monarch, swallowtail, blue, brimstone, sulphur, social. He recited a poem called "Eletelephony" that he'd always found funny: "Once there was an elephant/ who tried to use the telephant/ No! No! I mean an elephone/ Who tried to use the telephone ...." He began recalling some of the things he'd discovered in his *Enquire Within* book and was glad now that he'd spent so much time reading it, for it was like having stored a good supply of fuel for the winter, enough to keep his mind alight. He even found that he could actually *see* the book and flip through it at will (something he'd always wished he could do at night in the dark when he couldn't sleep). Mentally he turned its pages, reading about deserts and solar flares, lava and fireworks — all hot topics. Then he came to one page that showed a house on fire. The flames looked thrillingly real, even though Olivier knew he was just imagining it. And yet ... he saw two boys in the picture, and one seemed to be pulling the other out of the burning house, and ... that's when a door of the locker was thrown open and a brighter light flooded the room. With it came a trickle of warmer air. The door that had been opened was not the small outside door they had come in by, but a much larger one that led out of the locker and into the palace. The image of the boys and the burning house vanished from Olivier's mind, and he watched as the Emperor strutted in, followed by Pistachio and ... Peely!

The Emperor was now wearing several cat fur robes and clutching the outermost one to him with mittened hands — mismatched and grimy mittens, naturally. It was a long-haired, black and white robe, stuck with pieces of scotch tape and wads of gum, and flecked with squirts of mustard. He also had on several hats, some with earflaps, and one that looked like a tea cozy. Pistachio, not dressed for the extreme cold of the locker but no longer on his leash, was hopping around and running up and down to keep warm. Peely was dressed in his usual way, with the one torn sock hanging around his ankle, exposing that peculiar mark — or was it a scar? — that Linnet had mentioned earlier. Olivier noticed that the weather on his socks was drizzly and dreary, and Peely himself presently looked more bluish than orange. He was shivering and glancing guiltily around, especially at the rows of frozen children, and most especially at his frozen friends.

"They … they can't hear us, can they?" he asked, his voice quavering.

"Of course not, what did I tell you? Not too bright, are you? *Sniff, sniff.* I'll say it again louder, so listen up. These items here before you cannot feel a thing. They cannot see or hear or speak. Why, they're dumb as posts. We, the royal and magnificent we, aren't cruel, you know. We are kind, generous, intelligent … ahhh, how true, where was we … ah yes, *sniff*, you must tell us, that is *I*, me, you understand, which one of these thieving, conniving brats has my toy?"

"Um, you're sure it's yours?"

"Mind your own business, I mean, *yes*, always has been. Lost, misplaced, that sort of thing. Get it for me, like a good br— *child*. I'm sensitive, you understand. I'll break out in a rash if I have to touch either one of them. Yech, the very thought. They're slimy, aren't they? Oh, I know all about children, they carry diseases, they're filthy creatures, they'll give you warts if you pick one up."

"Well, no …"

"Don't be pert. No one dares to disagree with the Emperor. Do recall what you stand to gain. You were doing your duty to tell me about the toy, *my* toy, and how you saw these crooks run in here. You are unusually sensible for your kind. Didn't have to twist your arm *too* hard, did I? Spilled the beans, what? So-o-o-o-o, you get the reward I promised. I'm going to let you have a lick, instead of a lickin'." The Emperor tittered at his little joke.

His very little joke. Olivier himself was not so amused. Peely had betrayed them, and for what? A lick of ice cream!

"Life," exclaimed the Emperor, rubbing his mittened hands together. "This is your last chance."

No, don't, Peely, Olivier implored, but only with what expression he could muster with his eyes … and Peely was avoiding eye contact, as if he knew that Olivier could hear every word. It wasn't so much the remote, let the old fool have it. With luck he'd blow himself up or shrink himself down to his real size. No, it was that infernal ice cream of his. It might give those who tasted it endless life, which is what Olivier suspected it must do, but it took something away, too. He was sure of it. Something you needed to make that life worthwhile.

Peely reached toward him, hesitated for a moment, then hastily dug into the pocket where Olivier kept the remote and fished it out. The Emperor pounced. He snatched it out of Peely's hand and ran toward the door.

"Come," he ordered. "Look alive. Pistachio, get over here at once, don't touch that creature. You'll get fleas, *sniff*."

Pistachio had scampered up Olivier's leg, and then up his chest. He made a grab for Murray and pulled him out of Olivier's shirt pocket, then scurried back down with him. He zoomed past Peely and the Emperor, and was gone out the door in a shot.

Doubly robbed! The remote *and* Murray! Olivier was so indignant he was boiling. It's a wonder he didn't thaw himself out on the spot.

"Pistachio ... *stop*," the Emperor bellowed. "Did you see what he had? That worthless pen. I thought I had the defective thing taken care of. The most useless instrument I've ever owned. Bring that piece of garbage back here *right now*. I'm going to have it melted down and turned into a spoon. Might as well, it's so empty-headed. Do you know," he continued as he marched out the door, with Peely trailing awkwardly behind him, "that every time I tried to write an ode in praise of me, that so-called pen would only write the most appalling insults. Not only that, but it refused to write propaganda, I mean, *information*. It even refused to sign death warrants, um, birth certificates, that is." He was still grumbling and complaining when the locker door slammed shut, leaving the room in frigid silence once more.

Amazing, Olivier thought to himself, impressed with how bold and brave his pal had been, how he'd stood up to that tyrant. Murray *was* a hero, exactly like the kind he had wanted to write about. Now he'd been stolen again, and he was in even more danger, and Olivier couldn't do a darned thing to help him out. He felt like kicking something, and to his surprise, he swung his right leg back and *did*. The something behind him, said, "Ouch, *hey*."

"Linnet? Is that you?"

"*Yes*."

"Sorry, I didn't know I could move."

"That's okay. It's good to feel something, even a kick. Why d'you suppose we can?"

"Could be the warm air that got in when the door was open. I don't know, but thinking about Murray seemed to help. I still can't move, only my one leg."

"And we can talk. Let's *really* think about him, and all our other friends too. That could be the secret to getting out of this place."

"Good idea."

Before they could get going on this plan, though, the door of the locker opened again, this time more slowly and quietly. Then — *zip* — the smoke slipped in and was curling all around them and bouncing up and down and forming itself into cheery, warming shapes — a hot water bottle, an electric sock, a chili pepper.

"Smoke!" they both said at once, so glad to see it.

Next, the one who had opened the door entered, crouching as he stepped into the locker. It was the Shuk who had helped Olivier.

"Hush," the big man whispered as he walked over to Linnet, picked her up and headed back toward the door with her tucked, stiff as a statue, under his one arm. "Be right back," he said.

While he waited, and what else could he do, Olivier watched the smoke drifting in and around the rows of children. As it did so, it darkened in colour to a deep charcoal grey and dropped lower and lower to the ground, either from the cold or from the discouraging sight. Fortunately, and true to his word, the Shuk wasn't long in coming back, and Olivier soon found himself being toted out the door as if he were a plank of wood, carried as Linnet had been under the Shuk's arm. It was fascinating to watch the floor skim by underneath him. From this vantage, the smoke swam in and out of view, shark-shaped at first, then splitting up into a whole school of minnows.

They headed down a long hallway, made a turn and then another, and finally entered a room that was about the size of a large closet or storeroom. The first thing Olivier saw was a narrow green carpet that resembled an unrolled length of sod, and even smelled like it, fresh and earthy. On closer inspection he realized that it *was* sod. After he'd been placed upright on this, he surveyed the rest of the room, or what he could see of it, as he was still mostly frozen. He decided that it must be the Shuk's quarters, for there was a big sheet of bedrock in one corner, and in the other a sink that resembled a birdbath with a bar of soapstone sitting on its ledge. The room also had some unexpected touches. A window had been thrown open, and there were lawn chairs tossed around, piles of sand, a barbecue, an upside down pot of geraniums and a whole pile of baseball gloves, stacked one on top of the other.

The Shuk shrugged at Olivier's questioning look. "It has been very windy," he said, with that rumbly voice of his.

"Wind? Great." Olivier wondered if it was the same one that Linnet had called up earlier, and looking over at her, he saw that she was stretching and rubbing her arms and shaking the last of the freezing cold out of her hands and feet. Then the warm breeze that had been busily thawing her out swept over to him. Straightaway he felt as if he were surrounded by hot air vents, or stuck inside a huge hair dryer. What a relief — he didn't even mind the pins-and-needles sensation in his arms and legs as he began to thaw — and soon he was back to his old comfy self.

The breeze then cruised through the room one more time, picked up a baseball glove off the top of the pile, and blew through the open window, rattling the panes and waving goodbye with the glove as it went.

"Thanks for letting it in," Linnet said to the Shuk. "You saved us. My head was so frozen I couldn't manage it. I didn't even know it was still hanging around." She walked over to him and took his hand in her own.

The Shuk smiled shyly at Linnet. She marvelled at how small her own hand felt as it clasped his big stony one, and how warm his was. It was a bit dusty, too.

"You've saved my skin twice now." Olivier also moved over to him, which is when he noticed a star-shaped tattoo on one of the Shuk's biceps. No, wait, he thought, it was a fossil — how interesting. He didn't want to stare at it, and so continued, saying, "We don't even know your name."

"My name? Why, no soft-body has ever asked me my name before." He crinkled his grey brow, surprised. "It is … Ig."

A soft-body? Better than being called a busybody, Olivier supposed. "Ig? Is that short for Ignatius?" (He knew a boy at school with that name, except everyone called him Egg, and sometimes Pug, because being called Egg made Ignatius *pugnacious*.)

"No, Igneous."

"I should have known that. Nice to meet you, Ig."

"Young one," he said as they now shook hands (and he definitely had a firm handshake). "We Shuks need your help."

"You've got it. I don't know what I can do, though, the Emperor swiped my remote when we were in the locker. It's this really helpful device and it's going to be a lot harder without it, and treacherous once he figures out how to use it. Even worse, his ink monkey grabbed Murray again and ran off with him … and, well, you Shuks are so strong. Why don't you just toss the Emperor in that locker, and her, too, while you're at it?"

"I will tell you," said Ig. "He is a thief. He stole something useful from you, and he stole your friend. All the inkslingers, by the way, he has had locked up or broken so that no one can write anything against him."

Inkslinger! Murray would like that, but Olivier sure didn't like what he was hearing.

"From us, the Shuks, he stole the Birthstone."

"What's that?" Olivier knew what a birthstone was.

His was a diamond, because he was born in April. Surely this wasn't the same?

"It is a stone that came to our people out of the sky thousands of years ago. It is as black as night, and this big." Ig indicated how large the stone was, about the size of a soccer ball, by gesturing with his hands.

"A meteorite?" asked Linnet.

"Could be. The story goes that it thumped one of our ancestors on the head when it fell out of the sky, and woke him up. Before that we were nothing but piles of rock — no feeling, no life — that is the legend. True or not, the Birthstone is very important to our people. It is ancient and there are all kinds of beliefs attached to it. How it has healing powers, and so on. Me, I always thought those beliefs were nothing but a load of gravel."

"They aren't, are they?" Olivier guessed. "That's why the Emperor stole it."

"So it appears. I have no proof, but I believe that he is grinding it into a powder and putting it in his ice cream. This has to be what is going on. The Birthstone, it cannot last forever."

"That's what I thought. About the ice cream, I mean. The secret ingredient is a kind of preservative right, and it must have the same effect on whoever eats it. And if adults can live forever, who needs kids?"

"I do not believe the Birthstone is meant to be eaten," said Ig sadly. "It is too powerful. It is making his people sick."

"Why don't the Shuks stop him?" said Linnet.

"We would, gladly, but we cannot find where he has concealed the Birthstone. He claims he will return it in exchange for our service, but that if we try to get it back on our own, he will destroy it. That is how he keeps us under his thumb. The other Shuks do not understand that he is destroying it, anyway. They do not think it is possible."

"So you've looked for it?" said Olivier.

"Yes, myself and one other, my friend Mica, whenever we can manage it. We have searched everywhere, without any success."

"You think we can find it?"

"Young ones, I know you can. I have been watching you. You are both brave and smart."

Olivier grew thoughtful. "It's like the Stone of Destiny," he said. "It was stolen from the Scots and they got it back after hundreds of years. I read about it in my book."

"Hope it doesn't take us that long," said Linnet.

"It's also called the Stone of Scone."

"Mmm, sounds good," Ig said. He too was looking thoughtful, and began to dig in the pocket of his tunic. He then pulled out a whole handful of precious stones — pearls, rubies, emeralds — just like the buttons on the remote. He flicked several of these into his mouth and began crunching them like candy. "Want some?" He held out his hand to the children.

Linnet and Olivier declined politely, a little taken aback to see such beautiful jewels being munched like snack food, but also realizing that they themselves hadn't eaten anything for a long time. This must then have dawned on Ig, as well, for he said, "You must dine first, and then we will decide what to do. The Royal Larder is kept well stocked for the Empress. She eats ... much! I will take you, follow me."

At the promise of a meal neither of them was about to hesitate, and they readily followed Ig back out into the palace hallway.

As he walked beside the others, the smoke hovering like a dark and ominous cloud above him, Olivier was considering the difficulties that lay ahead. They had many obstacles to overcome here. How tough was it going to be, and how dangerous? He had to find Murray (before he got turned into a spoon!), and the remote — he'd need that for sure — and the Birthstone, and ... Peely. Yes, he had to find Peely, and *soon*. That star-shaped fossil on Ig's arm had reminded Olivier of something that was of vital importance. Peely had to be told about it before it was too late. *Both* their lives depended on it.

Fifteen

The hallway they proceeded along was high-ceilinged and wide and smelled unpleasantly sweetish. The farther they moved from the Shuk's quarters, the more gaudy the palace became. Greyish walls gave way to ones that were cotton candy pink and fuzzy peach and honeydew green. When Olivier ran his hand along one of these walls, a powdery substance came right off on his fingers and fine crumbs trickled to the floor. How safe were they in this building? He knew it was made of ice cream, but reckoned there must be more to it than that. It had to be combined with a more substantial material. They had passed under several ornate chandeliers, heavy with oversized crystal pendants, so the ceilings were stable at least. The walls also supported numerous portraits of the Emperor's ancestors. Fake, obviously. They showed him, and sometimes the Empress, dressed up in various historical costumes: the Emperor as Napoleon, with a big blob of raspberry jam on the epaulet of his uniform, or the Empress, barely able to fit in the frame, done up as Cleopatra, regal beak pointing skyward and hands clutching a snow cone instead of an asp.

Portrait followed silly portrait, each more ludicrous than the last. Olivier and Linnet had begun to nudge one another, grinning and barely able to contain themselves, until Ig gave them a warning look. In case someone spotted them, he had advised the children to pretend that they were prisoners and workers. They resumed glum expressions, and just in time, for a palace servant then rushed past them. He was carrying a large silver tray, and upon it there was a plate that was stacked high with ice cream sandwiches and an enormous goblet filled with a red, syrupy drink that spilled over the sides as he hurried along.

"Is that for her?" whispered Linnet after the servant had disappeared down the hall.

"No doubt," said Ig. "She will be kept busy while you get some food. The Larder is up ahead, that door on your left. You two go in and have what you want — anything, except ice cream. Don't be tempted. I will keep watch out here."

Silently they slipped in, and were flabbergasted by what they saw. There were shelves and shelves of fancy desserts — trifles, cheesecakes, puddings, pies — as well as donuts and cinnamon buns and sweet breads glistening with icing, cookies the size of saucers, candied fruit, Turkish delight, trays of chocolates, jars of jelly beans, huge bags of mints and toffee.

"This is rough," said Olivier. He knew they shouldn't be wasting any time at all in here, but the display was overwhelming. They'd grab a few treats and be on their way.

"Yeah," agreed Linnet, "where's the broccoli?"

"Let's see, hard to choose …" Olivier fired three chocolates into his mouth one after the other.

The smoke, which had skittered in behind them, mouse-shaped, now drifted up to the highest shelf and stretched out, reclining lazily on a plum pudding the size of a bowling ball.

Linnet reached out hesitantly for a macaroon, and before she knew it she'd polished off half a dozen, followed shortly by a butter tart, two eclairs and a caramel apple.

Olivier made short work of an almond flan, two pieces of angel cake, some date squares and, for dessert, a fortune cookie. He almost ate the fortune, too, only pulling it out between his lips like tickertape before he could chew it up.

"What's it say?" Linnet asked.

He stared at the tiny piece of paper. "Help."

"It says 'help'? *That's* supposed to be your fortune?"

Olivier's face reddened, because he suddenly thought of all the poor half-starved kids who worked in the factory, and who probably made these desserts too, their mouths taped over so they couldn't eat any. And here they were, he and Linnet, stuffing themselves greedily. "Linnet, we've both had more than enough, let's go. I've got to find —"

"Yummm." Her eye had fallen upon a gorgeous looking dessert at the far end of the larder. It was a large moulded confection, covered with a whipped vanilla icing and sprinkled with coloured sugar and gumdrops. It was so beautiful that it seemed to glow. "I *have* to try it. Just a little taste."

"Don't," warned Olivier.

"Why not?" She strode down to it and already had her finger poised to scoop up a generous sample. "It's irre-sistible."

"It's a bombe. *Don't* touch it."

"A bomb? That's silly."

"It's ice cream, Linnet. That's what it's called, a bombe, I know because my mother tried to make one once. Hers melted all over the place. It was a total mess and we all had a good laugh, but I remember the pictures from the cookbook."

"Exactly. If this was ice cream, it would melt." She was gazing longingly at it.

"Not necessarily. Not in this place." Olivier remem-bered the banana split that had earlier attracted Peely in that storefront window. "You know what Ig said about … hang on, *listen*. Did you hear that?"

"No. What?"

Olivier was certain he'd heard a muffled noise coming from behind a closed cupboard door. He walked over and put his ear against the door, and heard it again, a *mmph mmphh* sound. Linnet moved quickly back to Olivier's side, the enticing dessert forgotten, and gestured for him to go ahead and open the door. It was locked with a clasp, which he quietly unhooked. Then, clenching the door's round chrome knob, he gave it a yank. It sprang open and out fell something that was not only unexpected but … horrible! Linnet clapped a hand against her mouth to stop herself from letting out a scream, and Olivier jumped back in alarm. He could hardly believe what he was seeing. A mummy!

Freed from the cupboard, the thing scrambled to its feet and started hopping around, but in a way that seemed sort of familiar. *Mmmph mmnph*, it was saying, *mmmph!*

Getting over his initial shock, Olivier took a closer look and saw that the mummy was actually someone wrapped up in masking tape. It had been wound around and around this person, with only a small vent left under the nose for air.

"Mummies don't usually wear glasses, do they?" said Linnet. These had been taped over as well.

"I have an idea who this is. Hold still," he said to the mummy, and started to unravel the tape, beginning with a loose strand wrapped around the chin area.

A mouth emerged, which said, "Oh, man ... like wow, what a drag."

"Jack!" said Linnet, pitching in to help, beginning to unwind the tape around his right hand and arm.

Olivier managed to uncover his head, deftly removing the tape without pulling off Jack's sunglasses or beret.

"Hey, it's you cats."

"What happened, Jack? Who did this to you?" Olivier asked.

"Same old story, man. Didn't I tell ya, blame the messenger. It was that royal chick."

"The Empress?" Linnet was unwinding the tape from his other arm.

"Yeah. Hey, thanks." He tried snapping his fingers, although they were still tacky and kept getting stuck together. "So, like, I tell her there's trouble happenin' in

Squaresville. Some of the parents want their kids back, eh, what's goin' down here is not cool. That's my message, man. Can she dig it? No way. Clam up, she says, bring me some mocha ice cream with chocolate sauce. Baby, I says, skip it, you are TOO much already. You are one BIG chick."

"She wigged out?" said Olivier.

"You got it. Next thing ya know, daddy-o, I'm all wound up."

"Way to tell her, Jack," said Linnet.

"Hey, just doin' my job, baby." He himself had pulled off the rest of the tape by this time, and had begun to jive around, saying softly, "Doo-wah, doo-wah."

"Could you take a message to someone for me?" said Olivier.

"Lay it on me, man."

"It's for Murray, my pen friend. Pistachio took off with him, I don't know where, but you must be familiar with this place. You know the ink monkey's hideouts, I bet. Tell Murray that we're coming for him, and that no one's going to hurt him, but I've *got* to talk to Peely. It's a matter of life and death."

"I'm hip. I know that little inky dude. He's real cool. Your other pale pal, he's in the Banquet Room, saw him go in before I got dragged in here. Then I heard that Emperor cat in here fixin' him up an ice cream, yakking away to himself. Oh man, he *will* be a real gone guy if he eats that stuff."

Olivier looked grim. "Let's go then. Hurry!"

"Hold on," said Linnet. "Ig is talking to someone outside. Sounds like the Emperor."

They all crouched behind the door and listened. All, that is, except the smoke, which slid down from the plum pudding, slipped past them and then poured through the crack in the bottom of the door.

The Emperor was trying to get into the Larder, and Ig was blocking the way.

"Move, I say, there is something I must get, *sniff, sniff*. Out of my way!"

"Emperor! Down the hallway, look! Smoke … it must be a … a fire?"

"Smoke? Where … a *fire*! Help, help! Alert the guards. Shuk, do something, you fool. The palace will melt. Fire!!"

"This way, Emperor."

"Brilliant," said Olivier, as they heard Ig and the Emperor rush off down the hall. "Our smoke does it again. Okay, let's move it."

They rushed out of the Larder and headed down the hall in the opposite direction, Jack leading the way. After passing though an open foyer and ascending a wide stairway that led to the second floor of the palace, they arrived at a large set of double doors — the entrance to the Banquet Room.

"Catch ya later," Jack said, leaving them there and hustling off to find Murray.

"I sure hope so," said Olivier, but more to himself, as he and Linnet pushed through the doors.

"Oooh," Linnet said when they stepped inside, for the Banquet Room was sumptuously decorated with gold satin curtains, red velvety walls and a purple carpet, so deep and plush that they sank into it up to their ankles. Instead of windows, there were mirrors everywhere, which caught and reflected the light from yet another fantastic chandelier hanging in the centre of the ceiling — this one a dragon made of spun sugar. On one side of the room was a silver door, highly polished and also reflective. Even the banqueting table, also enormous, had a mirrored surface. And at the far end of the table, sitting with a huge silver dish of ice cream directly in front of him, and a heaping silver spoonful of it almost touching his lips, was Peely.

He was regarding the ice cream with distaste, as well he might, for it was deep black in colour. Evidently he was steeling himself to take a bite, and had been doing so for some time. So absorbed was he in this task, and possibly even a bit mesmerized by the strange dessert, that he didn't even notice Olivier and Linnet enter.

"Don't, Peely," said Olivier, moving toward him.

Peely looked up, and gasped. "Uh, I thought you guys were … I didn't *mean* to, honest, I — "

"Never mind, forget it. We understand. You haven't eaten any of that, have you?"

"Not yet. I'm going to, though." He gripped the silver spoon tighter. "You can't stop me. Why should you, what's it to you, anyway? This is my last chance. I don't want to … you *know*."

"I do know. I *know* that you don't die. But if you eat that black ice cream, I will. Or at least I won't be born."

"Huh?"

"Olivier, I think someone's coming," said Linnet. She had stayed by the double doors, keeping guard.

"Wallace Peele, you're my father's best friend," Olivier

said quickly.

"What! Your *father*?"

"You haven't met him yet but you will, in about a year's time. *Your* time. After you leave Cat's Eye Corner, probably, I'm not sure exactly when. Anyway, you become really good friends and play on the same teams — baseball, hockey — and, you know, do all kinds of neat things together. One of those things is haunting houses. Late at night you sneak out of bed and meet, and go into old abandoned houses and run around in them, pretending to be ghosts. Sometimes you take flashlights, and once a kerosene lamp."

"I'd never do that. I'm not brave enough. Besides, it's stupid."

"It *is* stupid. I can't believe my father did it. I guess that's why he told me about it. So I wouldn't do it."

"Olivier …" Linnet warned. She had her back pressed against the doors, trying to hold them closed while someone pushed against them on the other side, and then began knocking against them with a hard object.

"The kerosene lamp got kicked over and a fire started. My father was trapped, and hurt because he'd fallen through some rotten floorboards and broken his leg, and Peely, *you* saved him. You risked your own life to save my father. You ran back into the burning house when you heard him cry for help, and somehow you pulled him out."

"I *didn't*. I mean, I couldn't. That was some other kid named Wallace Peele."

"No, it's you, definitely. My dad said his friend had an unusual sun-shaped birthmark on his ankle. It was unique, he said, and unmistakable."

Quickly Peely looked down to where his torn sock was drooping, and there indeed was a faint sun-shaped mark on his ghostly ankle, an imprint left by the sock itself. Then he looked at the spoonful of ice cream. "Well ... then, if I do live, and all that you say happens, it's because I've eaten *this*."

"I'm not sure why you recover, and you *do*, but it's not because of the ice cream. If you eat it you'll only become selfish, like the parents whose children are trapped here. You'll save yourself from the fire, but you won't save my father."

Still staring at the spoon, Peely muttered something that was drowned out as the person who was banging and pushing on the door finally overpowered Linnet and burst in. It was the Emperor, brandishing a sceptre in the shape of an ice cream scoop. Immediately he began bellowing, "There was NO fire, it was a false alarm! Had to send that dratted Shuk to the quarry, have him beaten into dust. *You*, yogurt-face, eat up, I don't have all day. *Sniff*, what are you brats doing in here? I'll fix you!"

The Emperor hurled his sceptre onto the floor, then reached into his robe and pulled out the remote.

"No," shouted Linnet, as he pointed it at her and hit the opal button. She tried to dodge aside, but too late. A prickling sensation shot instantly up her arms and legs, and in a second she was rendered completely stiff and still.

"Ha ha!" The Emperor then wheeled around, selected a jewelled button randomly on the remote and hit someone who had just then appeared at the open door. It was

Jack, proudly holding Murray aloft, and with Pistachio perched on his shoulder.

"Hey, man, ohhh nooo, not again!"

The Emperor had pressed the topaz button, and all three of them were now miniature versions of their former selves. Pistachio screeched and chattered with fright, for he was already tiny enough. Murray was disgusted to find himself suddenly no bigger than a pin, and not only that, he was in a panic because he knew whose turn was next.

Olivier darted over to Peely, shielding him from the remote, while directing him to hide under the table. He then stood up straight and faced the Emperor. Staring boldly at him, he said, "Listen, you don't know what you're doing. It is very powerful."

"Yes, it *is* powerful, isn't it? As am I, now that I have this *and* the Birthstone." The Emperor let his thumb wander lightly and teasingly over the buttons on the remote, which was trained directly on Olivier. Then, with a quick jab, he pressed one — the diamond.

What happened next caught everyone by surprise. Olivier vanished. He was *gone* — erased completely from their sight.

Sixteen

The Emperor inspected the remote with delight. This fancy doohickey had such extremely useful functions! Already he was thinking about how easy it would be to rid himself of useless children — the sick ones, the ones too exhausted to work any more and especially the defiant ones who refused to co-operate. Why, he could solidify them, shrink them and turn them into marketable figurines … and turn a nice profit, too. They'd make such charming mementos. He could sell them to the parents, and as figurines they'd be less bothersome than the noisy, pesky originals. Naturally there were a few he'd have to get rid of altogether, like that frightful boy he'd just eliminated. With the Birthstone almost used up, this doodad could save him from losing control over his Ice Cream Empire. Indeed, he'd be able to fix those few troublemaking parents for good, not to mention any renegade Shuks.

If the Emperor hadn't been quite so taken with the remote and had been paying a little more attention, he might have noticed the arrival of the Empress, and then given her some warning to watch her step, or to duck when Peely leapt out from under the table and lobbed his whole, uneaten spoonful of black ice cream in her direction. Peely was in fact trying to hit the Emperor, but he was so upset about what had happened to Olivier that his hands were shaking and the shot went wild.

"My dear," the Empress pronounced, swanning into the Banquet Room, "I understand you were looking for this … OCH!" As usual, her nose was tilted upward, and the ice cream missile that Peely catapulted from the spoon hit it with full force, and a good portion of that cold black dessert shot straight up her nostrils, plugging them both. She had been carrying a tray upon which sat the bombe from the Royal Larder. With the ice cream up her nose, the Empress staggered forward in surprise, then tripped over the sceptre that the Emperor had tossed onto the carpet. The bombe was launched. It sailed through the air, caught the edge of the dragon chandelier and then exploded, exactly as if it were the other kind of bomb. The chandelier rocked back and forth, then crashed onto the table, causing both it and the mirrored surface of the table to shatter. Shards of glass and sugary pieces of dragon and dollops of icing and gumdrops were flying everywhere. As well, a flattish black object that had been concealed in the bombe bounced off a corner of the table and landed right in Peely's hands.

The Empress was sprawled on the floor, snorting and gasping like a beached fish, and the Emperor, who had a big gob of icing dangling from his chin, turned to her and said, "What a terrible mess you've made. It's disgusting, and you know I HATE mess, *sniff, sniff*. Why are you grovelling like that, my dear? It's not very dignified." She gave him a sour look, but before she could think up a nasty retort (and the Empress *was* a mite slow in the thinking department), he had noticed what Peely was holding and demanded, "Give that here." He aimed the remote at Peely's chest. "Or else!"

Peely was examining the object, which was round and smooth and hard. It was Olivier's puck, he concluded, but he was puzzling over how it had gotten buried in that bombe. One thing he did know — if the Emperor wanted it, he wasn't going to get it. What did it matter if he got cancelled out by the remote, anyway? He wasn't going to live much longer, no matter what Olivier had said about his father and the old house and the fire. It was only some screwy story he'd made up so that Peely wouldn't feel so bad.

"Not on your life," Peely said, and glared defiantly at the Emperor, much as Olivier had done.

The Emperor's eyes widened in surprise, which was gratifying to Peely, but it wasn't really because of what he'd said. Jack and Murray and Pistachio had only that moment arrived at the Emperor's ankle and had mounted an attack. It had taken them some time to get there because the carpet was so thick that it had been like blazing a trail through a shoulder-high stand of dense purple grass. On top of that Jack had to hold his nose because the Emperor's socks were so smelly.

"Peee-yew! Oh man, phew. Okay, ready? Like, chaarrrge!"

The Emperor's socks also had lots of holes in them, so that when Jack dashed toward his ankle with Murray extended like a lance, they made contact with bare skin.

"OW! OUCH!! OOH!!!" The Emperor started hopping around on one foot, and then he began slapping at himself because Pistachio, flea-sized, had jumped off Jack's shoulder and was scurrying around under the Emperor's robes, pinching and biting him.

"You *fool*," laughed the Empress, who was struggling to get to her feet and dabbing at her nose with a used candy wrapper. "*Not* very dignified, ha!"

Linnet had been standing stock still all this while and helplessly observing everything. She'd been horrified when Olivier had disappeared, and very angry, and frustrated because there was absolutely nothing she could do. It had helped to see Peely so defiant, and to know the others were bravely doing what they could, and to hear the Emperor and Empress snapping at one another. But without Olivier ... and *then* she felt a warm breath against her ear that she knew wasn't one of her breezy helpers.

"Linnet, I'm still here," whispered Olivier. "The diamond button, it made me invisible. I'm going to get the remote back, it'll be a cinch."

Yes! she thought, so relieved that Olivier was safe, and so tickled to see the Emperor jumping around as if his pants were on fire, that she would have whooped out loud if it were possible.

The ankle-jab that Jack and Murray had inflicted wasn't all that serious, but the Emperor kept grimacing and moaning and carrying on. Jack had run with Murray to take cover behind a large vase, in case they got stomped on, and Pistachio had bailed out, too. He'd scurried up a side table and climbed into a silver goblet to hide.

Olivier knew he had a great tactical advantage in being invisible, and it was time to use it. He moved swiftly into the path of the Emperor, intending to snatch the remote out of his hand. But the Emperor was so distracted by his pain and suffering that fumble-fingered, he hit the sapphire button by mistake. Suddenly Olivier appeared again, fully visible, his fingers almost grasping the remote.

"You!" The Emperor pulled back his hand.

"Olivier!" shouted Peely.

"Give me that thing," insisted the Empress, and she was the one to grab the remote out of the Emperor's hand. "I'm sick and tired of playing second fiddle to you … you *slob*. So what is this thing, what's it do?"

"Don't touch any of the buttons, please don't," said Olivier. She had too firm a grip on it for him to snatch it away from her.

"Please, is it? I didn't hear pretty please with sugar on it, now did I? So I'll just press this one." She pushed the ruby button, and one of the mirrored windows shattered and a torrent of broken glass cascaded noisily to the floor. "My! That was fun." She spun around, pressing the emerald button, and hit a soup tureen, which then leapt off the buffet and, with its little legs churning, dashed out of the room, spilling strawberry soup as it ran. She clicked the pearl button and a marble bust of the Emperor done up as Mozart melted into a sizzling glob. She then turned to the Emperor himself and aimed the remote at him.

"My ... darling," he stuttered, while staring at her dumbfounded, his pain completely forgotten.

Without the slightest hesitation, she pressed the diamond button ... and he vanished. The Empress said smugly, "Cleaned that mess."

Her satisfaction was brief, however, because she soon felt an invisible force trying to wrest the remote out of her grip. She didn't know, of course, that she hadn't got rid of the Emperor entirely, and she let out a fearful scream as the remote was plucked out of her hand and began to float away.

"Emperor," Olivier shouted, "Look what I have. The Birthstone. Catch!" He reached into his pocket for the puck and hurled it in the Emperor's direction — or at least where the remote was floating in midair.

"*Oof!*" they all heard, and Olivier knew he'd hit his mark. He ran and dove for the remote, which the Emperor had dropped after being smacked with the puck. Olivier scooped it up, scrambled back onto his feet and began clicking buttons like a channel-surfer.

First he made the Emperor visible again, in case he got up to more mischief, and then he froze him for the same reason. Then he froze her too, the Empress, just as she was sneaking up on him. Next he thawed Linnet, and then he restored Jack and Murray to their right size. *And* he restored Murray to his rightful place in his shirt pocket, giving Murray a welcoming tap on the cap as he did so. Pistachio, who was cowering in the bowl of the goblet, had to be coaxed out.

"Don't be frightened. None of this was your fault," Olivier said to him. "You were trying to save Murray when you stole him from me the second time. Right?"

"Yeah, man," Jack said. "He'd saved a pile of writer dudes. He was hidin' them in this way-out pencil case."

Or, as Murray later confided to Olivier, *I was confined in a wooden box with a bunch of rude mechanicals, a rustic crew of inkhorns and lowly, chewed-up eraser-heads, and they were none too sharp, either. Imagine!!*

Emboldened, Pistachio stuck his head up over the rim of the goblet and then climbed out of the cup and down the stem, onto the table.

"This won't hurt, I promise," said Olivier as he pressed the sapphire button. The minuscule creature instantly became a tiny creature once again. Then, chattering excitedly, he ran over to the edge of the table and leapt back onto Jack's shoulder.

"He likes you, Jack," said Linnet, flexing her hands, enjoying the sensation of being able to move again.

"What a gas. Hey, we're gonna be a team."

"So will you and my dad," said Olivier, turning to Peely, who was looking more confused than ever.

"I thought *this* was your puck," he said, holding out the round black object that had been hidden in the bombe.

"No, Peely, that one is really the — "

"Birthstone," said Ig, who had appeared in the open doorway. "It is much reduced in size, but thank the heavens it still exists. I knew you would find it. I have been telling my people so already."

"It's *yours*?" said Peely, at the same time that Olivier said, "You're safe!" and Linnet said, "You escaped from the quarry!"

"Mica was the one ordered to take me there," he smiled, "my *loyal* friend." Ig glanced meaningfully at the Emperor and Empress, both of whom had been caught in unbecoming stances and with idiotic expressions frozen on their faces. Barely hiding his distaste, he then continued, "We have been busy, no stone left unturned, or I would have come to find you sooner. You will never guess, but there were aggrieved and rebellious parents on that bus tour, disguised, pretending to be otherwise. While you were keeping these two occupied, they took control of the factory and released the children. Now, with the Birthstone back in our possession, we Shuks can heal the other parents and undo much of the damage. They must learn to treasure it, not devour it."

Ig then held up his hand and said to Peely, "Young one, please."

With perfect aim, Peely threw the stone right into Ig's hand.

"Good one," commented the Shuk.

"Take this, too," said Olivier, tossing Ig the remote. "It'll help fix things. Something tells me I won't be needing it any more." (Although he wouldn't have minded being invisible again, especially at school.) Something told him that Sylvia's troublesome guests wouldn't be needing it either. Ig caught it in his other hand and nodded his agreement.

"Unless ... what about those kids in the freezer?" Olivier asked.

"Taken care of," said a girl who suddenly appeared at Ig's side.

"Sharon!"

"Hi, guys. Told you I'd help. C'mon over to the window and see for yourselves."

Everyone followed Sharon over to the one mirrored window that the Empress had broken, and looked out.

"See," she said proudly, pointing down at a crowd of children, some milling around, some simply standing looking dazed, and a few others even throwing sticks (two) for ViceVersa to chase. "With some Shuks' help, I found the controls and turned off the freezer, and we got all the children outside, where it's warm — it's like summer. There's even new grass growing. You can see it over by the river."

"Your windy pal is having a blast, Linnet," said Olivier.

"Yeah," she chuckled. "There go the baseball gloves from your room, Ig."

"Ah, yes." A cloud of the gloves were hovering in the air, and some children were leaping up trying to grab them and slip them on. While craning their necks upward, several of them even noticed those standing by the window, and began waving and shouting happily at them.

As everyone waved back, Sharon said, "More kids are joining them."

"From the factory. I recognize some of them," said Olivier.

They continued to watch as more and more children appeared on the palace grounds (many easing duct tape off their mouths), along with a large group of Shuks, palace servants and parents from the tour. Everyone was talking and hugging and laughing. It was a heartwarming sight, but one that Peely couldn't bear to watch any longer. Sadly, he turned away from the window just as another Shuk, a very worried one, ran into the room.

It was Mica, the Shuk that Olivier had seen Ig speaking with earlier.

"Out, Ig," Mica said. "Children, everyone, flee! The palace is crumbling. Melting. The north tower has collapsed already. Out!"

"Yikes, run!" said Olivier.

Linnet was already heading for the door.

"I'm not going anywhere," said Peely, so quietly that no one heard him.

"Young ones, stop," said Ig. "Not that way. It is only for us." He indicated Mica, Sharon, Jack, Pistachio and himself. Then, reluctantly, he included the Emperor and Empress as well. "Mica, we will have to lug these two outside. Then I will reverse their present state ... to match their fortunes, also now reversed."

"What other way *is* there?" asked Linnet.

Ig indicated the silver door at the other end of the banquet room.

"How does it open? There's no handle on it or anything."

"Looks familiar," sighed Olivier. "I guess we're going home."

"Not me," said Peely.

"OHHH, YOOO HOOOO! Children, there YOU are!! I've been looking EVERYWHERE for you ... you little SCAMPS!!!"

"Okay," said Peely. "I changed my mind. I will go."

Yes, hard to believe after all they'd been through, but it was Oscarella Vivid, grinning inanely and colourful as a rainbow. She strode purposefully into the room, brief-case in hand.

"We were just leaving, sorry," said Olivier, walking hastily toward the silver door, with Linnet right behind him.

"NOT yet! Wait, WAIT. I have something for the pasty-faced one, a present from that nice MR. KNUCKLE-BUCKLE."

"Uncle Truckbuncle, you mean? A present for me?" asked Peely.

"YES, that's it. GOODNESS, but I've been TRYING to GIVE it to you!! Chasing you ALL over the countryside … so, HERE it IS!!"

"Um, ma'am, the palace is about to — " said Ig.

Oscarella Vivid waved her hand airily, shooing away Ig's protest, then set her briefcase on the floor and unsnapped it. The lid flew open, and as she foraged around inside, a number of items tumbled out: — a rub-ber boot, a broken ukulele, a recipe book entitled *1001 Ways to Cook Parsnips*, a stringless yo-yo and a shaved ookpik. "AHA! Got it, found it, I KNEW it was HERE." She began pulling and tugging at a piece of cloth in the case and finally yanked out a strange looking coat, coloured blue and green and brown and red and patterned with silk rivers and woolly forests and velvet skies. "You MUST try it on!!"

Peely was extremely reluctant, but he didn't have much choice, as Oscarella was already slipping it on him, first one arm, then the next, then up over his back, adjusting, straightening, then, "OH! Perfect fit. It's YOU!" She stood back, admiring him, beaming.

"Gee, Peely," said Olivier, "you look like … a … a … hippie!"

"Hang on, I know what it is," said Linnet. "A *life* jacket."

"You wanted one of those, didn't you?" Sharon was smiling. "You look fantastic in it."

"Yeah, man. *Cool* threads," said Jack.

"Peely, your hands," said Olivier.

"I've … got a rash, or something." Peely was staring at his hands, which had become a fleshy pink colour. "It's spreading, I think." He reached up to touch his cheek, amazed at how flushed — and solid — it felt.

"A soft-body," said Ig. "But not as soft as you were, I believe. Young ones, it is time."

Even as the Shuk said this, there was a tremendous crash and the floor itself began to shift and sway beneath their feet. The warm wind that had been swirling around outside poured through the open window and began gusting around the room with a swiftly escalating force. Ig hit the sapphire button on the remote, and the silver door slid open. He raised the hand that was still holding the Birthstone in triumph and gratitude … and farewell.

"Goodbye," they all said, "goodbye," as the wind, growing stronger and stronger, could no longer be resisted. While all of the others rushed out of the Banquet Room, with Ig and Mica bearing away the Emperor and Empress like statues (ugly ones), Olivier and Linnet and Peely found themselves being swept beyond the threshold of the silver door.

"Where's the elevator?" shouted Linnet as they began to fall and fall down a pitch-black shaft.

"And where's our *smoke*?" shouted Olivier back.

All Peely said was, "WHHHAAAAAAAAA!!"

Seventeen

At first they plunged straight down very fast, but then they slowed almost to a stop and began to float sideways in slow motion for a while. After that they rose upward again, then wafted downward, and then they were tossed around a bit as if they were nothing more than dried leaves caught in a windy eddy. At one point Linnet flew right past Olivier and waved. A short time later he saw her floating on her back, hands behind her head, completely relaxed. He didn't see Peely at all, and when he looked around for him, that's when he realized he *could* see. Not too far below, a light was glowing faintly and he and Linnet were drifting down toward it.

Then all of a sudden their fall accelerated, as if gravity had taken hold again. Olivier felt himself tumbling faster and faster until he crashed down and landed on something that was both bony and soft.

"Ow! Get off, will you. You're on my leg."

Olivier shifted over. He saw that he'd landed partly on Peely and partly on a bed. *His* bed at Cat's Eye Corner. Or ... no, wait, it wasn't his room exactly. The bedside lamp, which was the light he'd seen from above, wasn't the same as his. This was one of those corny old-fashioned lamps with a picture of Niagara Falls imprinted on the shade. Not only that but the bedcover had a Wild West design, with cowboys and lassos and bucking broncos, and there was a poster of a really old hockey player on the wall. Rocket Richard? Boom Boom Geoffrion?

"I didn't know you were a Canadiens fan, Peely," he said.

"You never asked. What about you?"

"Leafs. No question."

"What are you two talking about?" Linnet had landed on one of the pillows at the head of the bed and was sitting up and looking around, puzzled. "What happened to your room, Olivier? Sylvia must have done some redecorating while you were away. It looks , I dunno, peculiar."

"That's because it's my room," said Peely. "My room at my grandmother's place. I'm back, and ... and you're not going to believe this, but I'm better. *Cured*. I can hardly believe it myself, but I feel *terrific* ... healthy, strong, I could run around all over the place. Say, there's this neat tire swing out front, I've been dying to go play on it, I mean — "

Linnet smiled. "It's true. You look great, Peely."

"You're not a ghost any more," said Olivier.

"Never was. But you guys are."

"Holy mackerel." Olivier stared at his hands, shocked, because his skin *was* beginning to fade.

"I can see right through my arm!" said Linnet.

Peely was about to respond, then paused, listening. "Voices," he said. "Someone's coming down the hallway. Sounds like my grandmother and — I can't tell, probably the doctor again. You two better hide. Golly, what will I say? I was so sick, and now I'm not at all." He tugged off his Life Jacket and hid it beneath the covers.

"I bet you won't have to say anything, Peely. Your grandmother will be so thrilled and everything, she won't even think to ask how it happened. We'd better make ourselves scarce, Linnet. Let's hide in the closet."

"We already *are* making ourselves scarce," she said.

They both slid off the bed and headed toward the closet, and then were astounded to find themselves walking straight through the closet door.

In a second, Olivier pushed his head back through the door and said, "Take care of my father, eh, Wallace Peele. In case you forget about all this, or think it was just some hallucination or dream you had when you were sick."

"You bet, Olivier. Holy cow, I'm going to have a best friend, I can't wait. But … you and Linnet aren't going, are you?"

"Who knows? Anything can happen in this house."

"*That's* for sure," Peely laughed.

Which was when Peely's grandmother entered the room, as he was laughing, a sound that she hadn't heard in weeks. Olivier ducked his head back into the closet, but not before he caught a glimpse of a slight woman with soft white hair and an extremely pleasant and kindly face. He also saw the look of astonishment on that face as she rushed toward the bed.

"Och, sweetheart, what's happened? You look … *bonny*. I cannae believe it! We thought we'd lost ye, my Peely Wally." She touched his forehead, then ran her fingers along his cheek. Tears sprang to her eyes, and eagerly she embraced him, holding on tight, lest this was some trick and her beloved grandson began to slip away from her once again.

"Gramma!" was all Peely needed to say.

"*Hooray*," whispered Linnet, as she and Olivier stood inside the closet listening. They heard a lot of sniffling and excited murmuring, and then, although her voice did seem to be growing fainter and fainter, they distinctly heard Peely's grandmother say, "Your parents, dear, I know you didnae want me to tell them how ill ye were, I know I promised not to, but I *had* to, and och, they had no idea. Thought ye were malingering … *tsk*, 'tis nae excuse … time they grew up, the two of them, I told them that too … aye, they're here, waiting outside … came as soon as they could … in a state … so very sorry about leaving ye, ashamed they are … and they promise to …"

Her voice then faded out completely.

"To what?" said Oliver. "What do they promise, did you catch it?"

"Nope. But it better be good, after abandoning him like that."

"You can say that again. I wonder why we can't hear them."

"Push your head through the door again. They're so busy with Peely, they won't notice."

"Okay." Olivier then whammed his forehead into the back of the closet door. "Ouch."

"Guess that didn't work." Linnet tried not to laugh. "Say, do you smell smoke?"

"Oh no, what now?" Olivier was rubbing his head.

Then they both said at once, "Smoke!" Followed by such things as, "How did you get here?" "We missed you." "I can't see a thing." "Where were you?" "Where are we, for that matter?" "Let's get out of here." "Yeah, but the usual way, no more walking through doors for me."

Olivier opened the door a crack, and the smoke zipped out and skimmed around the room, as if delighted to be back. The smoke wasn't the only one.

"All *right*," said Olivier. "*My* room this time." He took a quick look at his hands, which were nicely solid and visible once again, and then wandered around in his room, checking everything. All was in order, even his *Enquire Within Upon Everything*, which still lay open on the dresser. Gingerly he closed it, surprised at how warm the book felt. Then he retrieved Murray from his shirt pocket, and their notebook.

Once upon a time ... Murray began, without further ado.

"Um, just a sec, Murray. Looks like Linnet wants to get going, I'd better say goodbye." He set Murray and the notebook down on his bed.

Linnet was standing by the window. "It's dawn, but which dawn? If it's the same day, I'm supposed to meet Fathom before lunch."

"I'd like to see Fathom again. Sylvan, too." Olivier was thinking about how he had seen at least one of his friends recently, and it had been extremely helpful, but that wasn't the same thing as a good visit. He then yawned hugely. "After I get some sleep."

Linnet grinned at him and said, "Super, but when you come to see us, don't bring any ice cream, please. I don't care if I ever see the stuff again. Say bye to Murray for me, he seems preoccupied." She then opened the window, stepped out and, with a quick wave, climbed down the Boston ivy vine that clung to the side of the house. She landed lightly on the ground, then was off and running into the woods.

Olivier picked up Murray and the notebook. *In the beginning …* Murray wrote. A brisk knock then sounded on his bedroom door, and Olivier said, "Sorry, Murray, someone's here. Be right back." He set his pen friend on the bed again and walked over to open it.

It was Slyvia, looking as sly and interesting as usual. "Why, Olivier. Good morning. Nice and early, isn't it? I was wondering if I'd find you here."

"Hi, Step-step-stepgramma. Any reason why I shouldn't be?"

"Hmmn … no, I suppose not. I've come to invite you to breakfast. I've made something *special*."

"Really? I think I need a bit more sleep. Why don't you leave it on the table and I'll get it later."

"I'm afraid it will melt, dear." She seemed a little disappointed, but then her eyes lit up. "Our guests are gone, you know."

"What happened?"

"The Poets." Her eyes now widened in alarm. "They got out of my room, and dearie, the fur was flying, let me tell you. You have never seen two stately personages move so fast in your life. Practically shredded they were! They were becoming tedious, anyway. Food fights *every* night, ice cream snowballs flying everywhere, breaking mirrors, haven't a dish left in the house, flattened my toaster (that Lord Nose must have sat on it), ate all the nifty little sandwiches I made for my bridge club, and not only that, but I caught them trying to steal my jewellery. My emeralds, rubies, diamonds, sapphires, pearls. Do you know, I found my purple purse in the kitchen completely emptied out. The nerve!"

"I'll say. What frauds."

"Too right, my dear."

"Say, Step-step-stepgramma, I've been meaning to ask you something."

"Yeesss?"

"Do you know anything about the former owners of your house?"

"Indeed I do. I bought Cat's Eye Corner from an elderly Scottish woman. Very good-natured person, if you like that sort." Sylvia gave a little shudder of distaste.

"Why did she sell it?"

"As I understood it, she had this terribly ill grandson, who made some sort of miraculous recovery while he was staying here with her. When the parents, who were abroad, came to fetch him home, he didn't want to leave her. Apparently she was so fond of the child she decided to sell this place, if you can imagine, and move in with them. They bought a new house for the four of them — in your neck of the woods, Olivier, now that I think of it. The parents, who were a little on the flighty side, I gather, had a change of heart after almost losing the boy, and began to dote on him." Sylvia shuddered again. "But that was all a long time ago."

Sylvia turned to leave and then said, over her shoulder, "Once you've had your breakfast, why don't you come down to the basement and give me a hand? I'm going to have a yard sale. Curious, some of the things I've discovered down there … a sticky pink coat, a conch shell, an ice cream scoop as big as a broom … fascinating. Oh, and before I forget, a lovely letter came from your parents. Simply delicious!" she exclaimed, as she moved off down the hall.

Olivier sighed and closed the door. He walked over to the bed, pondering all of what Sylvia had told him. He picked up his friend once more, and without any delay, Murray began, *In a land far far away* …

Another knock sounded on the door, this time a quieter *rat-a-tat-tat*.

"Er, Murray," Olivier interrupted, and then, noticing how hot his friend was becoming, set him down hastily. "This won't take a minute, I promise."

Olivier hurried to the door and opened it. "Gramps!"

"Ollie, good mornin', son." He reached over the threshold and gave Olivier a big hug. "Want to play some road hockey?"

"Hey, I'd love to, Gramps, but ..."

The old man then reached into his pocket and pulled out a puck that looked *very* much like the one that Olivier had left behind in the collapsing palace.

"Where did you get that?" he said.

"Dinner. It's a bat burger. That Lord Nose fella tried one and he broke a tooth on it, heh. By jiminy, son, can ya dig it, are ya hip?"

"I'm hip, Gramps. I dig it the most," Olivier laughed. "Okay, first there's some writing I have to do," he glanced significantly over at Murray, "then I promised to help Sylvia clean the basement for her yard sale, then —"

"No rush, Ollie. I'll be working in the garden. I got some flowers planted in that wreck of theirs, and that stone fella's fixed up, too. Found him a new head. Granite, good and hard."

"That's igneous rock, isn't it?"

"Don't rightly know, but he sure is a fine sight. Come when you can, eh?"

"I will, Gramps."

As the old man shuffled off down the hall, Olivier watched him fondly, knowing that the shuffling was mainly for effect — Gramps could play a mean game of road hockey. He then turned back to Murray. He feared he was going to be in deep trouble if he didn't soon help the anxious author get on with his story. Murray had obviously gotten over his writer's block. But then something else caught Olivier's eye. It was the smoke, circling and circling above the book, in a way similar to what

Bliss did when he was settling down for a catnap.

"Smoke," Olivier said, "you want to go home, too, don't you?"

The smoke began circling faster, which Olivier took to be a yes. He walked over to the dresser and grasped the edge of the book's cover. He couldn't remember what page Mount Vesuvius was on, but that didn't seem to matter, for the book instantly flew open and the pages riffled back and forth until finally settling on the one that was wanted. The smoke zoomed up, nuzzled Olivier briefly, then dove into the picture, vanishing into the open crater of the volcano. Slowly Olivier closed the book, giving the cover a little pat before turning back to Murray.

"Boy, did you see that?" he said, retrieving his pal yet again, and readying the notebook. "That smoke was the real hero."

What! I . . . you . . . what!! Murray was fuming and spluttering.

"I mean, you know, the smoke did help us a lot."

That airhead? Give me a break! No, don't . . . you've given me enough breaks already. I do hope you're finished running to the door every two seconds. If you're ready, my boy, perhaps I can get on with composing my exceedingly important work.

"How long will it take, Murray?"

Is this an interview? Good to practise, I suppose. Let's see now, I usually write in longhand, and ohh, ten years should do it.

"Ten years? I'll be an old man by then. I've got stuff to do today." Olivier yawned again. "What's your novel going to be about, anyway? Our adventure?"

Why, yes, lad. How I fought off that gorilla, how I outwitted that Vivid person, how I defeated the Emperor and Empress, how I found the Birthstone, how I saved all those children, how I stood up to that terrifying ghost.

"Wait a minute, that's not how it happened."

I'll reshape the material a little, naturally. A few revisions, some tinkering, you know. That's how we writers do it. You wouldn't understand, Olivier, not being in the profession yourself.

"No, I guess not. Still … um, Murray." Olivier looked away shyly, and then asked, "Who are you going to dedicate your book to?"

Why, to me, of course. I'm surprised you had to ask.

"What? You can't dedicate the book to *yourself*."

Why ever not? I'll be doing all the work.

"I'll be doing some. Giving you support, bringing you cups of ink."

Wel-l-l, maybe I can work you into the acknowledgements somewhere.

"Thanks a lot," Olivier groaned. "You're a real character, Murray, no doubt about it." He shook his head and smiled at his friend, and then he yawned, and again, several times in succession.

Good, that's settled. Let's get started, shall we? Once there was a brilliant, dashing, staggeringly handsome, and brave young …

Unfortunately that was as far along in his story as Murray got. Olivier couldn't resist any longer. He was having trouble keeping his eyes open. He leaned over a bit, and then a bit more, until finally he keeled right over.

His head hit the pillow, he snuggled into his soft, warm, wonderfully cozy bed, and before Murray could write the word *pen* with a glorious flourish, our hero was sound asleep.

About the Author

TERRY GRIGGS is the author of a previous book featuring Olivier, called *Cat's Eye Corner*, which was shortlisted for the Mr. Christie Book Award and the Red Cedar Award, and was a Canadian Children's Book Centre "Our Choice" selection.

Terry Griggs' adult publications include a collection of short stories, *Quickening* (Porcupine's Quill, 1991), which was shortlisted for a Governor General's Award, and the novels *The Lusty Man* (Porcupine's Quill, 1995) and *Rogues' Wedding* (Random House, 2002). Terry was awarded the 2002 Marian Engel Award by the Writers Trust of Canada, in recognition of a distinguished body of work by a female writer in mid-career. Terry lives in Ontario, with her husband and son.